The Autobiography of

CORRINE BERNARD

A Novel

ALSO BY KATHLEEN NOVAK

Do Not Find Me

Rare Birds

The Autobiography of

CORRINE BERNARD

A Novel

Kathleen Novak

THE PERMANENT PRESS
Sag Harbor, NY 11963

For information, address:
   The Permanent Press
   4170 Noyac Road
   Sag Harbor, NY 11963
   www.thepermanentpress.com

Library of Congress Cataloging-in-Publication Data

Novak, Kathleen, author.
   The autobiography of Corrine Bernard: a novel / Kathleen Novak.
   Sag Harbor, NY: The Permanent Press, 2018.
   ISBN: 978-1-57962-540-5
       1. Middle-aged women—Fiction. 2. Self containment
   (Personality trait)—Fiction. 3. Man-woman relationships—Fiction.
   4. Life change events—Fiction. 5. New York (N. Y.)—Fiction.
   6. Psychological fiction. 7. Mystery fiction.

PS3614.O9265 A98 2018
813'.6—dc23   2018005297

Printed in the United States of America

dedicated to my daughter, Jenny, and—
my lifelong friend, Carrie Colburn

For well they knew, the parters in all evenings
Druid and Roman and the rocked Phoenician:
The blood flows one imposed way, and no other

—JOHN FREDERICK NIMS
from "Parting: 1940"

Dear Reader,

I want to set the record straight here: lots are cast in life.
One side of the street basks in sunlight, the other settles in shade.
My sweet Maman never understood this.
She put an extra lamp in the corner and called it a well-lit room.
But we were in the shade. There is no mistake on that.
Dwarfed by taller buildings and left to the northern light,
    our lot had been cast.
I have my tales to tell, but few of them are cheery, I warn you now.
The severed heart beats wildly beneath the floorboards.
Do you hear it? I do. I always do.

CORRINE MICHEL BERNARD

PARIS

~ 1 ~

I was born the night before the Nazis entered Paris. The next day their army marched down the Champs Elysees and hung its flag from the Arc de Triomphe. The French did not oppose them. Perhaps they never quite believed such unenlightened louts could occupy a blessedly poetic place like Paris, France. Or perhaps they were outnumbered. History tells us both.

Parisians followed the French government out of the city, loading into cars and trucks, wagons and carts, pedaling bicycles or hurrying on foot, all moving heavily but surely away, abandoning their furniture and linens, most of their mementos, and almost all their hope. I have no idea where they traveled. It was long before I knew such flights in fear and the ready search for anywhere.

In the midst of all that fleeing and bullying, my *maman* brought me home from the hospital to her rooms above a boarded boulangerie. I did not cause her difficulty. I squinted but did not blink, she said. I fixed myself on her and sucked her milk eagerly, waving my tiny clenched fists. That was how I began.

In Maman's story of me and the onslaught of Germans, she always detailed her window box, planted a month before with scarlet geraniums and purple pansies, violets, and ivy vines, easy flowers that held on throughout my first summer, the curfews and sirens, the worries and peculiar realities of war outside her door. "We lived behind the blossoms, me and Mimi," she'd say and actually look happy, as though it hadn't been a time of terror and loneliness, and she hadn't been left an unwed woman with a baby. Or maybe she had wed. My father was a soldier, she said. He died defending France, she repeated often, though I suspect he may have fled with the others seeking survival. I never knew him and rarely cared. Maman said his name was Michel Milot and so she named me Corrine Michel Milot. In that way, I have carried him with me, for what it has been worth. But even without husband and father, we spent my first summer behind the blossoms. She nicknamed me Mimi, a small dear name that did not indicate my difficult lot.

My birthday on June 13, 1940, was the first of my unfortunate legacies. Thirteen steps leading to the gallows, thirteen witches to form a coven, thirteen disciples at the last supper. A child in the neighborhood wouldn't come to have cake on my birthday one year. His overtly Catholic mother held to such things. Judas was the thirteenth disciple, after all. And though the boy's refusal did not hurt my feelings, his fright settled on me nonetheless. "Goodness," Maman said, "there is a thirteenth day of every month. And the cake is so pretty. Look, Mimi, I made it pink." I learned early not to disregard the shadow of the number thirteen.

Poverty was another legacy, though our condition was not so dire as it might have been. Maman did not have me out dancing on street corners for coins. We were not so thin we took sick in winter. On the top floor of our dark building the heat rose to find us, and Maman loved to knit whatever she could to arm us against the cold. We were poor like our neighbors were poor. Wartime poor, I suppose, luckless but trying. Maman watered our soup and made bread out of whatever she could get. She stood in the ration lines and came home with small parcels a fraction of what she had hoped. I grew up poor enough to watch for every meager opportunity, every broken toy tossed to the street, day-old sweets or a generous expression on any stranger's face. I learned immediately to take everything I could get and to never be satisfied. That is the legacy of poverty.

And then, too, I was born on a Thursday. I was not yet in school when Maman first recited the nursery rhyme: *Monday's child is fair of face, Tuesday's child is full of grace, Wednesday's child is full of woe, Thursday's child has far to go.*

I asked, "Where is far, Maman?"

"Oh, this is good, Mimi. Far is good," she exclaimed, elated. "You will have adventures. You will know queens maybe. See bright birds and far beaches. Yes?" She nodded again and again, her sweet young face, my maman in her twenties, always imagining, her eyes making an effort to stay merry no matter what deprivation she endured. I wish you could see her, gray eyes and dark curls, flushed almost always with excitement or some kind of exertion, the three flights of stairs, the reach to our tall cupboards, the many things to do in every single day.

The legacy of Thursday's child troubled me for years because of Maman. She remained my constant, patient and encouraging, as if life would soon be more, as if all her ebullient good nature would manifest the miracle and there we'd be, the two us, in well-lit rooms with a bountiful table and new wool skirts. As if our lot could be cast in a different direction. I did not want to go far from her. I did not want to be Thursday's child, born as the Nazi army marched in to take over Paris, born without a father and poor, and with, as prophesized, so very far to go. I did not choose that. Whoever does.

The war overshadowed my first ten years. Even when it was officially over, even when Paris celebrated in the streets and we went off Berlin time and our worst fears lifted, it was not over. We were still poor. The city was still struggling, lacking in food and morale, politicians arguing over who had been right, where to put the blame, rebellions surfacing here and there. But I learned of those things later. At the time, I was a child and, though the Germans were in command until I started school, I really did not think much about them. My bed was piled high with simple cloth quilts Maman had constructed out of any scrap she could find, this and that, and tied with the strings that sometimes wrapped her groceries. She unraveled an old scarf and knit me socks, cabled and creamy like the milk we drank so rarely.

During those years of occupation, life continued despite the Germans and their high steps, their rules and straight backs and tightly creased uniforms. As much as possible, the people in Paris just went along anyway, shopping where they could, popping into cafés or bars, holding hands, seeing theater, strolling about. There were undercurrents of rebellion, Maman told me later, horrific acts against the Jews and heroic acts to save them, secret networks of intellectuals who knew the answers. But Maman and her friends were neither heroic nor rebellious. They were young and energetic, trying to make the most of their situations. They shared bicycles to run about the city and stood in ration lines together, gossiping as they waited.

As a small child, I played with Maman's wooden spoons and her hand-me-down pots. I banged them and waved them like weapons to and fro. Maman scolded me, laughed, and taught me silly songs. I was not unhappy then.

But I was watchful. I understood so young that I did not have the freedom to throw even the slightest crumb to the wind. Have you seen hungry sparrows, feathers unkempt and eyes darting? Odd, unattractive birds with very little in their favor? That was my early childhood. I was a skinny, scrappy girl, wild-eyed and watchful.

~ 2 ~

The red bumps on my arms appeared just when I started school. A boy in my class noticed them immediately yelling, "She has spots," in a panic. "I can't sit by her. She has a pox!" Our teacher immediately picked him up by his ear and dragged him to the back of the room with some admonishment that I did not hear, because by then, the other children had all turned their eyes on me, afraid and clearly repulsed, their small bodies stiffened as though to ward off whatever awful thing I had—pox, measles, even leprosy. Children see everything and know nothing. The spots were not significant, I have had them forever. But at school, I was immediately marked.

Weeks later, or maybe only days, a different boy, Marcel was his name, found me alone in the cloakroom, stalling there because I had no friends. He pulled a crumpled bag out of his satchel and let me peek inside at his hoard of chocolate bonbons, a most wonderful sweet I'd tasted maybe twice in my short life, bites merely, gifts from my godmother, Claire. And now this rough boy with his front tooth already missing and his hair shaggy like a street urchin was in front of me holding a bag of them.

I met his eyes to ask if I could have a piece, but he snatched the sack away. "Show me your underpants." He raised himself larger. Just saying the words had made him important to himself. He held the bag of chocolates behind his back. "Show me."

I flipped up the skirt of my cotton dress high enough, then dropped it again, my eyes steady on this boy Marcel.

He shook his head. "That's not enough for a chocolate."

I turned and flipped the back of my dress and thrust my butt out just a little in his direction. Then I wheeled around fast, grabbed the chocolates, and ran away, through the classroom and down the polished, slippery hallway to the girls' bathroom, where I closed myself into a stall and took stock of my earnings. I counted six chocolate bonbons and ate them all, savoring their different fillings—a berry one for sure and two all chocolate, a nut in one, and the others vanilla cream perhaps. I closed my eyes in that dim bathroom stall and rolled the candies all around my mouth, licked my fingers, and listened for any posse on my trail. But nobody came.

The bathroom window opened at a slant high on the wall, so that we could never see out and the outer world could not see in. Through that window I heard the high squeal of a large truck braking, backing down the narrow alley, coming to haul away bad children, I thought, chew them up and swallow them forever.

When I had finished the candy, I peed, washed my hands, and returned to the classroom. I found my desk and slid in, waiting for Marcel to tell everyone I had stolen his candy. But candy was not allowed in school and, apparently, Marcel had no friends either, because he told no one and the teacher's lesson on basic addition went on as planned. I listened with solemn concentration, riveted to the chalk numbers she wrote on the board. I already knew basic addition and some basic subtraction as well. I knew that there had been six chocolates in the bag and now there were none. The one paper bag had been pitched into the metal trash can in the girls' bathroom. Nothing was left. Nothing equaled zero.

Marcel waited outside school for me, demanding that I return his chocolates. "You stole my candy," he hissed through the gap in his teeth, "and you'll pay for it too." He had such an awful face really. I kept my distance and continued walking home, but he followed. "You're a thief," he yelled to me, and I laughed at him. I picked up my pace and skipped along between pedestrians ambling in the late afternoon light.

"I loved those chocolates," I called to him and let myself be absorbed into all the passersby.

That night I lay in bed thinking about chocolate, the sweetness that wasn't too sweet and the way each one of the six bonbons melted in my mouth and covered my tongue. I thought about how much I loved having another chocolate after the first and then another. Then I began to wonder about the trade. A look at my underpants, plain and worn thin, the elastic stretched so that the legs hung baggy. Why did that boy Marcel offer his chocolates in exchange for a look at my plain underpants? I fell asleep with that wondering.

In the morning, I woke up knowing my own answer. That boy wanted to see my underpants because I was a girl and he wasn't. There in my corner of our apartment, under the steep angle of the roof with the torn flowers of the wallpaper dancing above me, I decided that this too was basic arithmetic. Like adding two numbers. My underpants could get me chocolate bonbons. Or more.

Marcel thought he would trick me and keep his sack of chocolates, but that was where he was wrong about me. That's where many people over many years have been wrong about me. I do not walk away empty-handed. Even at six years old I knew that about myself.

~ 3 ~

My early years at school stay with me mostly as an elusive blur of obstacles and boredom, poems I memorized, hours I daydreamed, and faces that came and went, like Marcel with his chocolate bonbons, standing outside the school and yelling feverishly that I was a thief. Poor Marcel.

Very clear is my memory of the route I took to school, just a short way along one narrow street, the buildings coming right out to the edge of the road with near crumbling walls left over from many centuries, gray and uneven, elaborated with vines and the like. I thought them as grand as the castles in one of Maman's fairy tales. Walking past these places, I imagined myself an explorer and a spy, an heiress to the kingdom and a writer of complicated stories that took hundreds of pages to tell. Often I was escaping tragedy. I'd dart in and out and look over my shoulder, taking large steps but remaining inconspicuous so that I could not be caught. Little did I know.

I did not have friends in those early years. Boys liked me some because, in certain situations, when they had a coin or a candy worth the trade, I would show them whatever they wanted to see. Marcel might have been surprised to know what I was willing to reveal as I moved through primary school. Even so, I believe I frightened them all. Boys, girls, some teachers, and I think that was only because I did not fear repercussion. At home Maman would find a good side to anything I did or wanted to do. Her scolding amounted to a mere finger wag and a laugh. We had so little. If I engaged in a bit of mischief, what of it? I was not incorrigible. I was, as I look back, independent. I'll say it that way.

I did not laugh often or join in or follow along or share stories in school. I kept to myself. I read books and scribbled numbers and thought about what I could do to find a better life than the one my poor maman had stumbled into, doing mending and ironing for her rich neighbors to pay her rent and drinking cheap wine with her jolly friends who, for the most part, had even less than she did. I thought about the characters in books who took to the road or the ocean, who found treasures and long-lost rich relatives and whose true identities pulled them out of misery.

In my fourth year of primary school I had a teacher who slipped me books to read, Jules Verne, and Charles Dickens, *The Adventures of Perrine*, and *Jane Eyre*. She watched me through her thick eyeglasses and encouraged me in my fantasies. She wore a heavy ring the color of her eyes. She called it jade and when I asked about it, she told me her mother's brother had traveled to China and brought back these stones, pale green and mottled, rare in France, she said, but not in China. Her uncle had also come back with stories of girls who had the bones in their feet broken and then their feet wrapped tightly such that they would never grow and the girls would never run away and men would find them dainty and delicate like ornaments.

She told me this from behind her wooden desk strewn with children's papers, which her hands sorted the way I'd seen my mother's hands shuffle a deck of cards, with purpose and an elegant strength. My teacher's hands were bony with long fingers and groomed nails, and on one of those fingers the enormous jade stone slid ever so slightly whenever she moved. These customs are passing now, she went on, but think of it, Corrine. Feet only so big. She placed her hands inches apart and peered through her lenses at me.

In my brown oxfords and cotton socks, my toes wiggled restlessly for days afterward. Walking to and from school, I began to notice details of the men and women bustling about in post-war Paris, and this is what I saw: men wore flat, sturdy shoes like I did. Some women wore plain boots and walked in free strides, but others did not. Their skirts were narrower, their shoes high-heeled, their hair pulled back or curled. None of them had small, wrapped feet, but they walked in measured steps anyway. The other thing I noticed was that the women in narrow skirts and high shoes attracted me, fascinated me. They had airs of some kind and some had smoothly painted faces. Often I couldn't take my eyes off them. And neither could the men.

Women like my mother and her friends did not have the resources or inclination for airs. They were busy surviving and one pair of flat, plain shoes or boots had to suffice, no matter what their private fancies. My maman, in fact, felt proud that her boots had no ripped seams or worn holes, that she had managed the few coins needed to keep her soles and heels intact.

I was not sure about the arithmetic in all of this. What was gained and what was lost. My pretty mother marched around Paris making do, her hair clean and her eyes wide. But did men notice her? I think they did not.

~ 4 ~

The books I read early on told me that men and boys took great risks, even courted danger. They kept their own counsel, rarely deterred from their destinies. They were, I discovered in one story after another, just like me. I so identified with these determined and adventurous characters, that I thought myself one of them. A few girls also made their own way in the world, orphaned, mistreated, and unflinching, like Jane Eyre or Perrine in her makeshift island hut, but they were the exception—wise and watchful, as I was. And later I found other women characters who were extraordinary, even in their inevitable tragedies.

That is what I wanted. To be extraordinary, to have wealth or power or fame. I wanted the winds to rage, the earth to split before my feet, the riches of the East to be found in my old wooden chest.

A girl who desired a wide world as I did, and had decidedly different opinions from other girls, did not make friends readily. I watched my classmates put their heads together with intimate ease, tell secrets into one another's ears, cupping their hands over their mouths protectively so the rest of us could not hear what they were saying. These girls almost never ventured off alone, but huddled in pairs and small groups, giggling often and with much spirit, sharing little tokens of their austere lives—hard candies and frayed ribbons and rings they made of scraps of twine.

Girls in life did not seem to be like Jane Eyre or Perrine. They weren't solitary or abandoned, but jovial and busy. In class they were quick to respond and show how much they knew, their hands shooting into the air to see who would be first and best. I behaved like the boys, who sat silently scrawling with their pencils or staring off out windows. I knew the answers, but they were too obvious to say. So I kept to myself and formed my own ideas and made my own way.

I remember one child whose mother came by for tea with Maman. The girl went to another school, but was my age at the time, probably seven or eight, and carried a doll named Francine with her, clutching the toy's cloth body and constantly kissing its porcelain head. "What do you play with her?" I asked.

The girl's eyes watched me with concern and she gripped the thing tighter.

"She's my baby," she said.

"So?" The pink lips on the doll's face were slightly chipped.

"I feed her and put her to bed and dress her. She's mine," she added.

"What if I want to take it on a ship to England?" I took a step in her direction.

"Her name is Francine," the girl defended. I remember that silly doll's name while I have long forgotten the silly girl's.

I also remember how much I hated the child's smug possessiveness, her surety that the doll was hers and hers alone, her grip on the thing so fierce that I could not wrench it away. Though I tried. She yelled for her mother and started to cry and, in a torrent of bad good-byes, the two were gone within minutes.

My mother looked so dismayed. "Oh, Mimi," she said, near tears herself. "Do you want your own dolly? Do you want me to ask Auntie Claire?" She searched my face.

"No, I don't want a doll."

"Then why did you try to take hers?" She had gone to her knees to be on eye level with me. "Why would you do that?"

"She said it was hers."

"But it was hers, Mimi."

I shook my head. "I don't think that way," I said. And I meant it. The world was large with everything in it. I would take whatever I found or whatever came my way. But it would not be mine. Very little ever has been.

~ 5 ~

In the last year of primary school, I set my eye on a small curvy girl who had moved in from some other part of France. Her name was Stella Cordeau, and she was placed toward the front where I watched her for many hours each day. She read the assignments and penned her notes and concentrated on the chalkboard as if it revealed the very word of God. Stella did not raise her hand to call out answers like most of the girls in class. Her feet, in scuffed boots one size too large, held together flat on the floor. Her socks were baggy and not quite white, her fingernails chewed, her brown hair braided down her back. She should have struck me as plain and unworthy. She certainly struck the other girls that way, for I noticed they did not reach out to encircle her.

Stella arrived a month or more after school began and slipped into her assigned desk just ahead of me and did whatever the teacher wanted us to do. At lunch, I saw her pull a cloth of cheese and bread out of her coat pocket and nibble at them while she studied the lumpy grass of the school yard.

I waited until a rainy day. It was mid-November and the flowers blooming in street gardens and window boxes had begun to wither. The rain was cold, I remember, because my hands were red, blotchy, and wet. I found Stella Cordeau sitting alone on the hallway floor and slid down beside her. "I'm Corrine," I said. "My maman calls me Mimi." I had never offered that information to anyone at school.

Stella smiled, and when she did, her whole face changed, became light and rosy, bright as a star. She had rather full features, luscious I would say now. "My cat is named Mimi," she returned.

I explained that my maman had wanted to include letters from my father's name and how he had died in the war and that I lived now only with my maman who sewed and ironed to pay our rent upstairs of a boulangerie. Stella watched me the way I had been watching her, with great interest, near zeal. "I am so sorry," she said at the end of my story.

This surprised me. "Why?"

"That your father died."

"Well, maybe he didn't," I contradicted and saw her bright face darken.

"You think he didn't die?"

"What if he ran away when the Germans came?"

Her eyes opened wider. "You think so? Why would he?"

I shrugged. "We don't need him anyway. We're fine without him."

"My papa lays bricks." She wanted to defend some type of familial order I felt. "It's important that every brick be set down so perfectly that the whole row is level and the building will last for centuries." She never took her eyes off me. "It's very important work," she repeated.

"Does he read?" I kept my eyes on her too. "Books and papers and such?"

Stella nodded slowly, as if not quite sure. Then she saw that I had registered her hesitancy. "He tells me stories." She smiled at the thought.

"Probably good enough," I responded and stood up and smoothed my skirt and walked away. Stella Cordeau had looked pretty and sweet to me in those weeks I had watched her in her desk as she listened and tried so hard. But her father did not read. Moreover, she could not remember that he did not read. If I had befriended her just then, if she had become the friend I never had, then the two of us would be considered *les filles stupides* perhaps. I would lose the power of my aloof autonomy at school and for what? For Stella Cordeau's perfect glow and companionship? No. I had to say no.

For the rest of that school year I continued to watch her only from a distance. Some boy chose to love her in the spring, and the two of them sat together whenever they could. I saw them holding hands near the school gate and bending their heads close together the way the groups of girls did.

I don't think I ever regretted Stella Cordeau. Still I was disappointed that someone else had figured out how to love her.

~ 6 ~

I suppose my lack of friendships worried Maman considerably, because—next to me—friends were her reason for living. She had friends from school and friends from the neighborhood and friends who were her sewing clients. Everyone Maman met seemed to want to be her friend. Even shopkeepers. Her friends, mostly young women then, popped by at all hours to have a story and a laugh. They brought treats now and then or Maman served them little cups of whatever she had on hand—coffee or homemade liqueurs, teas from dried plants—and in a flurry of conversation they would escape from the rest of life. At those times, I saw that Maman even escaped from me.

Often after school I'd sit squished in my favorite corner near her sewing machine, braiding scraps of fabric just because and listening to Maman leave me for a friend's world, some love gone awry or a soufflé that failed, the landlord's demands or the stresses of hard jobs. Like the silly girls at school, my dear maman and these women sat close together in confidence, their voices traveling up and around, punctuated by guffaws and high laughter. That's how it was. I didn't find them silly, though, because I knew Maman to be solid and reliable and unwaveringly kind.

After the incident with the doll named Francine, Maman stopped inviting her friends to bring their daughters along on visits. She never troubled me about it. I believe she thought my independent spirit would be beneficial to me in the long run and my ferocity as well. At least that is what I have concluded looking back, for she never pushed me to be other than what I was and she never burdened me with visiting children and their treasured toys ever again.

Maman had one favorite friend who was not robust and poor, but delicate, reserved, and wealthy. My godmother, Claire Bernard, adored both Maman and me and brought us tasteful niceties whenever she visited—a bottle of toilette water or lavender powder, lace-edged handkerchiefs of the finest linen, a bottle of champagne to toast an occasion. Maman swooned over these gifts. They elevated her—the refined fabrics and airy scents, the taste of rich chocolate and aged wine—and gave her the sense that she belonged in such a world, even if briefly.

As I grew older I would sometimes calculate that we might have eaten far better for weeks on the money Claire spent for one lovely treasure, a bottle of perfume, for example, or a tortoise shell comb. But I think Maman never did such calculations. A starched linen *mouchoir* tucked into her dress pocket gave her all the dignity she needed for days on end. And I suspect Claire knew this.

I remember the Claire of that time so clearly. She moved smoothly and coifed her hair smoothly. If Claire wore a pink-and-white flowered dress, which I seem to recall, then her shoes would also be pink and she'd have a thin strip of pink ribbon on her hat. She sat on the edges of chairs, not ready to run, but relaxed and straight, perched comfortably as a sweet bird on a limb. That was Claire.

Maman and Claire were born in 1919, just as World War I ended, when France hoped it had crippled Germany forever and the countries of Europe were busily rearranging themselves like ladies on a train. As my early years were lived under Hitler's occupation, theirs unfolded in a time of recovery and freedom. When they were children, Paris was the center of the civilized world, they said, brimming with artists and writers and jazz musicians. Ernest Hemingway and E. E. Cummings came and went, as did F. Scott Fitzgerald, Count Basie, and Josephine Baker, and it was in this atmosphere of energetic possibility that their childhood years passed.

But there was another darker bond between them too, because both had lost their mothers before they could remember them. Claire's mother ran off, she said, and never looked back or wrote. She left behind a closet of clothes, a row of custom shoes, and two young children aged one and three. She took with her a full-length fur coat and framed photographs of her babies. Claire's father never knew where she went. Or, if he did, he never told his children.

Maman's mother died just months after she was born, but to her, that death was as incomprehensible as Claire's mother's abandonment. How did a robust woman in peacetime Paris become so ill so suddenly? It never seemed right—or believable.

Maman had no siblings to share her loss. Claire had her brother, Charles, a belligerent boy two years younger, the kind of child who invited ridicule. For years Maman and Claire laughed about the young Charles, his pants often too tight, his gait awkward, his tendency to cheat on his assignments and steal from his classmates. After secondary school, he'd gone off to America, where finally people seemed to accept him, at least enough to make him rich in his own right at an early age. He bought and sold things, Claire explained, but then she'd start to laugh again and so would Maman. "Can you imagine?" they'd say. "Who would know?"

I pictured a fat little man with sinister eyes sneaking his way into American business, stealing from them the way he'd stolen pencils and erasers from his classmates. He was a caricature to me then, and maybe he always was. Even when I married him. Even when I watched him die.

At some point, of course, they had to take him seriously. That is what great fortune does—it encourages a certain faith or respect. He succeeded, didn't he? Would a fool be able to purchase an apartment on Fifth Avenue in New York? It was a fair question to ask.

~ 7 ~

I met Marguerite St. Louis in secondary school. She arrived like an alien princess, nearly six feet tall and large boned, fluid in movement as though her muscles gave no resistance, as though her bones undulated with the unseen moisture in the air. She wore glasses, the kind that are cut thick, so full of correction that nobody knew where she was looking or what was registering in her wide, brown eyes. If I met Marguerite at this point in my life, I'd likely find her a mystic, and even back then, at age fifteen, I found her magnetic. Elusive and disturbing.

Her family had just resettled in Paris then after years in Morocco, where her father held a position with the French government. In Paris, Marguerite and her learned parents lived in a three-story apartment that they occupied in full. Her mother's piano took up one entire room and whenever I visited—and I always pushed to visit—I would stand for long minutes in that room with its piano, the walls painted an apricot color that was her mother's favorite, the windows dressed in sweeping brocade drapes. I can still see that room clearly and the perfect gleam of the piano and the high white ceiling above.

None of that mattered to Marguerite. She preferred the sparse apartment where I lived with Maman, stacks of fabric and sewing projects piled near the sewing machine, some poor man's soup ever simmering, potato and onion or the like, and our beds layered with homemade coverlets. She loved it all. Maman worked with her hands, that's what Marguerite loved, and Maman sang popular French songs and recited childhood rhymes that made Marguerite laugh. I understood from the first day I invited her home after school—this was before I had seen her family's three stories of luxury—that she would have happily moved in with us, set up a narrow bed next to my own under the eaves with that flowered wallpaper peeling and flaking, and tucked herself in under Maman's pieced covers. She aspired to this, this authentic romantic existence she perceived our lives to be.

Through Marguerite I saw the glow that poverty has for those who do not live it. Marguerite didn't realize that her lot had been cast to so much more favor than my own. No. She lamented her mother's jewels, her father's travels, their bountiful cupboard and maid and endless formalities, while she esteemed my mended dresses and wild hair and constant plotting for day-old sweets. She wanted to be me.

And I wanted to be Marguerite. This was the arithmetic of our relationship, this crisscrossed wanting. I waited hungrily for every visit to her apartment and she followed me home regularly just to sit with me on the floor and watch Maman cook and sew.

In Marguerite, I found then another person who read constantly and had an interest in talking about books all the time. We saw things differently though, so there was no end to the solemn arguments we had. She disdained Anna Karenina for jumping in front of the train. A waste of beauty and strength, she thought. I commended Anna for her dramatic gesture of despair, miserable life that she had. We discussed these things with passion but also restraint, so that our intense feelings remained in check. What of this, she'd say. I disagree, I'd answer. And so on.

Those two years that Marguerite and I coveted each other's life, my maman was beside herself with pleasure, and so made my companion ridiculously welcome. She knit her a scarf, I remember, a shade of red much like black cherries, which Marguerite wore every day I knew her, fall, winter, and spring. In the summer, she draped it across her bed in her cream puff bedroom of white and ivory, pale pink and that distinct color of apricot her mother so loved that it flowed from room to elegant room like the theme in a novel. The knit scarf was too homely for her bedroom, completely out of place, yet she flaunted it as a prize.

Maman also sewed us matching slips out of some thin cotton left over from a client's project, pale blue with delicate straps. Marguerite grasped hers to her chest and began to cry. "Madame Minot," she declared, "I love you." To which my maman answered that she loved Marguerite in return. Then Maman smiled at me, as though this were our shared feeling, this love for Marguerite.

But I did not love Marguerite. Maybe I wanted to. I'm sure I wanted to. But she was not mine. She was the kind of girl who held so many cards—money and connections and her own stubborn intelligence, her own romantic views, her keen eyes behind those thick glasses that saw as much as I saw but at a utopian angle, grand visions and belief in those visions. I could love her no more than I could the mourning dove that landed daily on our window ledge, a gorgeous soft creature that looked directly at me and blinked before it flew off to another window ledge across the way. Marguerite, I knew, would do the same.

After we completed secondary school, she traveled to see a relative in London and stayed. She wrote that she preferred speaking English and was learning to drive a car and had taken to smoking cigarettes without filters. She fell in love with a woman she met through her aunt, an aunt who herself preferred women, she wrote. "And I perhaps preferred you, Corrine," she ended. "Perhaps I should have been more clear."

This did not shock me. We'd often held hands. We'd kissed as French do, coming and going and in-between if the situation was right. As girls who spent long hours together in all seasons, we knew each other naked and flushed and possibly seductive as well, never comfortable companions, always on alert and ever attentive. Marguerite and I had edge and friction and, I would say, a disturbing oppositional play. We were to each other the constant reminder of what we wished to be and were not, what we wished to have and did not.

She sounds so interesting, doesn't she? And she was. The others at school left us alone with our crazy hair and heated discussions. As we continued to spend time together throughout those two years, I saw that even a person of privilege could behave with reckless abandon. Maybe not really reckless. Maybe a calculated abandon, more like tossing a hat into the wind. That was something I remembered later. When I lived high above one of the most expansive parks in the world and rode a gilded elevator to my rooms and possessed a closet of clothes as fine as Marguerite's mother had owned, I remembered Marguerite's abandon. Even now, I should say, I continue to emulate that kind of abandon. At any station in life, no matter the age or circumstance, one can toss a hat into the wind.

Of course, I can never forget Marguerite St. Louis. Over time I have become her in my own way. And perhaps these long years later she too thinks, ah Corrine, I have become *mon cher ami*. It's possible. I cannot help but think it is possible.

~ 8 ~

Before we finished school and before Marguerite left for London, I began to work in the boulangerie on the first level of the building where we lived. I stood behind the old wooden counter—flour on my apron, my hair wound into a bun—and parceled out loaves of *miche* and *pain de mie, baguettes, and brioche*. I was sixteen years old then and working in that boulangerie turned out to be the only job I have ever had. At the end of each week, I received an envelope with my name in perfect printing and the money I earned sealed inside. At the end of each day that I worked, I was allowed to choose two items from the remaining breads and pastries and take them upstairs to Maman.

I did not have the personality to sell anything. I have never been patient with people or interested in pleasantries. But the artistic sweets and loaves of every shape baked by Madame Roche and her two cousins pleased me such that I never complained. Not when my feet hurt or a customer argued over cost or boys from my school stopped in with their silly antics. I think I didn't smile, there in my floury apron, but I never complained and I counted change handily and the Roche cousins took to me despite my *comportement*, as Maman would say.

When I finished school, I increased my hours and Madame Roche gave me responsibility for closing in the evening, pulling down the metal gate, and locking up. One night just before I turned off the lights, a young man hurried in, asking me questions about this bread and that, his French tentative as he pointed and shrugged and selected two loaves, which I wrapped and tied while he watched me with much interest. "You are beautiful," he said. I nodded and handed him his purchases. Then he asked, "Will you have a drink?"

I looked at him for a long time before I answered. I didn't study him, but I took him in, and even now I can tell you that he was not tall, that his hair was very black and his eyes very blue. He wore a wool jacket that hung nicely, and he had shaved well and added some scent to his young, smooth face. He had a merriment to him that reminded me of Maman, an easy jolliness as he stood fumbling his wrapped loaves of bread and the small box of profiteroles he'd added at the end. Whoever said no to such a person? Whoever didn't go out to have a drink with him and see what he had to say and what journey he was on in his groomed and sweet-smelling life?

"My maman lives upstairs and is expecting me," I said in English to confuse him. Then I said, "Merci," and busied myself with some task, arranging the few remaining baguettes perhaps. He did not leave. He tried more of his broken French where he stood by the door and I continued working with great diligence until I heard the door open and close and glanced up to see him crossing the street slowly, laden as he was with the best breads in Paris and his disappointment in me.

It wasn't long after that when I traveled to New York to visit Claire and met her brother, Charles. And so I have thought, then and now, what would have become of me if I'd closed the boulangerie that night and gone to share a drink with the young man in the wool jacket? What if, as we might say about one turn of events or another? What adventures might I have known with that young man and his merriment?

It is always something to ask.
It is always something to wonder.

~ 9 ~

At this time, I think Maman began to wonder something similar. What was to become of her Mimi, her baby and dear? Was I to work in a boulangerie forever, clomping up the stairs in the evening with leftover sweets? We had no money for further schooling, which probably broke her heart. "You are too smart for *ficelle*," she'd lament or, "What did the baguettes teach you today, Mimi? Ah, these *cannele*. Geniuses, *non*?"

She inquired frequently about Marguerite who remained her beacon of hope for my future. Perhaps Marguerite's father could find me an embassy job. Perhaps Marguerite and I might form an office of some kind together.

"An office, Maman?"

She would shrug with bewilderment. "You are such bright girls. There must be something."

We had versions of this conversation many times. Then an hour or two later she would have an idea. "You might be tutors." "You might write letters and speeches." "Would you ever learn shorthand, Mimi?"

Somewhere in that year of my mother's fretting, Claire announced that she planned to move to New York to look after Charles. This too Maman could not understand, but Claire told her, "My brother cannot remain alone in America. Who knows what will happen to him?"

"But he's rich, Claire. He's successful now, and he's been there many years." Maman had poured herself a glass of wine, which she took in large, unapologetic gulps, her face flushed and sweaty. "He doesn't need you."

"He is my baby brother and money or no money, he is alone in America."

Maman continued to argue the absurdity of a sister influencing her thirty-six-year-old brother, especially Charles, who had never taken to suggestion at any point in his life. There was no need for Claire to go. Paris was home. And so on. But in the end, I believe Claire wanted to go to New York. She was single and wealthy and, no matter how much she loved Maman and me, Charles was family. And America was America, after all.

This was in December of 1957, the year I was seventeen and out of school. Before Claire left, we celebrated Christmas together. Maman knit her a foggy blue cardigan sweater of merino wool, staying up past midnight for many days to finish it. I brought pastries from downstairs and Claire gave us each a cashmere scarf, mine lemon yellow, a color you wanted to taste, and Maman's the pink of summer roses. We wrapped ourselves in them, and Maman cried the rest of the night.

A month or so later, Claire sent me an airline ticket to visit her in New York.

I asked for two weeks' vacation from the boulangerie, and because it was a slow season between Christmas and Easter, the Roche cousins let me go with their blessings, although I saw in their faces that they may have rather faced the guillotine than climb into a contraption that left the ground, disappeared into clouds, and hovered over the Atlantic Ocean for seven hours or more. The youngest cousin hugged me for a very long time, whispering *ça va, ça va* into my ear.

Maman seemed more optimistic. Claire had made the flight safely and Charles had gone back and forth several times those many years he'd been in America. So the odds were in my favor and the opportunity generous. I saw this in her face as she waved me away, the pink scarf looped around her as I had the lemon yellow one looped around me.

Claire's ticket put me in the front of the plane at a window. From the first rumble of the engines, I felt in my realm. The plane's wings stretched out behind me, the uniformed stewardess took care of my every need and after takeoff, the city of Paris, the French countryside, and the ocean all lay beneath me in endless bounty. I never closed my eyes. I saw ships and white caps below. We floated through enormous clouds and over thin delicate clouds and I was more free than I had ever been.

~ 10 ~

I did not dream that I would not see Paris again for nearly forty years, that the boulangerie would change hands twice and Maman pass away and all the paintings in the Jeu de Paume be moved before I would return. If I'd thought any of that, I might have wanted to fall out of the plane into the unforgiving ocean, plunge as the gulls did into the nearly black waters, and never surface again.

But I did not know. And the stewardess gave me champagne and the plane lowered toward New York City with its sky-scrapers, rivers, and tunnels, and all its millions of people going in every direction.

Now I can tell you the life that was ahead for me happened one hour by the next—singular encounters, fortunes or mis-fortunes, things I did and did not do, changes even in the weather. That is the surprise. That the future is only this street I cross, this feeling I have, this very lovely drink of twelve-year port. There is no plan. That is the surprise.

So I did not think about what I was leaving behind. My maman and her constancy. My little boulangerie of butter, flour, and chocolate, the old streets and old river winding through. I did not look back because I did not know that I had lost them. One hour was one hour. I was seventeen years old. And traveling.

I landed in New York in a light snow. It was midafternoon and the city hurried as Paris never did. The faces did not look familiar to me, nor did I see a single boulangerie on the long ride from the airport to Claire's. Thinking back, I believe I barely saw the sky.

MARRIAGE

~ 1 ~

Claire had already bought an apartment a block away from her brother, a space more splendid even than the three stories Marguerite's family occupied in Paris. The rooms were newly painted in pastels, so much like Claire, and carpets had been laid to match the walls. She had a blue room and a paler blue room and a pale gray room. But her rooms were mostly empty.

"Where is your furniture, Claire?"

She laughed. "It's coming, it's coming. Meantime I stay at Charles's. You too. We'll go soon to meet him, but for now I'll make us tea."

In her kitchen, larger than Maman's entire apartment, Claire had managed a table in front of a window and wooden chairs that might have come from a farmhouse in France. She said she'd bought them at an antique store in New York and laughed in delight at this.

I was tired from the trip, but I remember that day in its every detail. The clean white tiles on Claire's kitchen floor, for example. The thick gray living room carpet and the way my feet rocked slightly when I stepped on its thick pile, the one pink rose Claire had put on the kitchen table in a cut-glass vase, the kind of indulgence she always loved, and the glossed imperfect wood of the heavy farm table. I remember that Claire wore a winter white matching skirt and sweater, and a shade of lipstick the same color as her table rose.

It is with that same kind of detail that I remember meeting Charles.

After our cup of tea, Claire and I bundled up again for the one-block walk through the February dusk to the sixth floor of the building where Charles lived. A doorman greeted us as if we were royalty, and we rode upstairs in an elevator of elaborate brass and paneling. Claire rapped on the door to the apartment, a double door of grandiose proportion.

And there was Charles. The man of a hundred silly stories, the man who had once cheated for answers and pulled little girls' hair and stolen bits of money off his father's bureau. But this Charles standing in the doorway in a starched white shirt was not fat and his eyes were not squinty. He was only as tall as I was, with hair as black and eyes as blue as the man who had come into the boulangerie. But with none of that man's merriment. In a moment, in the time of one quick intake of breath, I felt the meanness, the powerful challenging mean-ness of Charles Bernard.

"You're Corrine." He had his hand on the door and I remem-ber that too, a thick almost muscular hand that should have belonged to a laborer not a man who bought and sold things.

"I am," I answered, and, without waiting for his invitation, I walked past him into his apartment. "And I'm so hungry."

Immediately Claire headed for the kitchen to talk to the cook. "Do you mind if I sit?" I asked Charles. "I'm quite tired."

He had followed me into his living room, its ceilings perhaps twenty feet high and its windows looking out to Central Park. I sat in a chair covered in heavy silk, patterned in gold, a color Charles appeared to favor, gilded frames and figurines, that sort of ornamentation everywhere. I took it all in, trying to ignore the man standing near me as he watched me absorb his wealth and taste. The drapes hung in folds on the carpet, proof that material meant nothing, that there was luxury here to spare, to hang in puddles of patterned silk.

When Claire returned, Charles went away until it was time to eat. He entered the dining room wearing more silk, a jacket sashed at his waist, and sat at the head of the table talking to Claire about the work being done on her apartment, new fixtures, custom cabinetry, all beyond my interest. Claire tried to include me, but Charles ignored her efforts and so did I. I didn't want to talk. I wanted to listen, to track his voice, the resonance and inflections, and to watch his cold eyes as they moved about the room. I focused on the meal. The cook served steak that night, sautéed rare. Every time I cut off a piece, a stream of blood trickled across the fine china plate.

After dinner, Claire excused the two of us and brought me to a guest bedroom where a fire had been lit in the fireplace and the curtains drawn. My one suitcase had been miraculously delivered to this room and placed on a padded bench at the foot of the bed. That is how Charles Bernard lived in New

York City. That boy everyone had scoffed. He'd shown them, is what I thought that night in the pale shadows of the perfect room where I was to sleep. He really had shown them all.

I did not sleep well. I awoke after only a few hours, at the time when in Paris I would have gone downstairs to work at the boulangerie. Beyond the apartment, New York continued to vibrate, never not busy. Soon I would come to thrive on that never-ending motion, but the first night in my wide bed down the hall from Charles Bernard, I heard only danger. A shriek of brakes. The speed of traffic. Urgent sirens. Even so, all of this called to me. I swear it did. As if nothing had existed before New York and Charles Bernard and nothing else would matter thereafter.

I did not return to Paris in two weeks as planned. Instead Maman flew to New York in April to see me marry Charles Bernard in his perfectly tailored tuxedo. He had insisted I buy a wedding dress at Bergdorf's with a veil to hide me until the very moment we wed. Charles understood drama, I have to give him that. The exact white flowers, the stone church on Park Avenue, the great crescendo of the wedding march played on both organ and trumpet that announced us as we walked toward one another. The reality of what we were and what we felt mattered much less.

I never liked Charles. But I loved his arrogance and intensity—and I loved the ease of his life, the money that came out of nowhere and went everywhere. That's what I loved.

He didn't touch me in any way before we were married. I'm sure he thought I would hiss and call it all off. I said just enough to him to get what I wanted and no more, and

Charles understood that. In his world of buying and selling this was exactly how things were done. No more was said than needed to be said.

"Are you in love with Charles?" a nervous Claire asked soon after I'd agreed to marry him.

"He's very interesting to me," I answered.

Claire frowned. "He is twenty years older."

I said, "I know."

"Well," she sighed to the room at large, "we'll be family anyway." She tried to smile.

~ 2 ~

Charles did not propose to me. First he recommended that I stay in New York longer than two weeks. Then he asked Claire to take me shopping so that I could dress the way he and Claire did, with attention to detail and quality, labels from France and Italy. Every evening when he returned to the apartment high above Fifth Avenue, he carried a gift. A string of pearls, leather gloves from Florence, chocolate bonbons, if you can believe. He gave me one sweater a week, all such fine knits I thought they would float on air. He came home with champagne and sweet liqueurs. Nothing suggestive. Nothing that could raise Claire's eyebrows. In fact, his gifts were much like Claire's had always been—tasteful, luxurious, and terribly expensive.

That was how he wooed. We would meet at dinner when he would hand me a gift, wrapped beautifully, and then the three of us would eat the extravagant courses that his cook prepared for us and drink some rare wine that he'd had sent over from his man at the liquor store. Charles had a man for everything—for his cheeses and meats, his imported shoes and fine clothing, his hair, his ties, and so on. Each luxury had a specialist and those specialists catered to Charles, part of his close network of men who knew what needed to be known. During these long dinners, Charles might ask us questions about our day, about the progress on Claire's apartment, about the news some of the time. Does this sound dull to you? Let me tell you, it was not dull, for at that time there was always this passionate tension, this near animosity between us. Who can understand such things?

Then after a month of gifts and long dinners, he handed me a jewelry case with an enormous diamond ring inside. "Well, Corrine?" he asked. I don't believe he smiled at me, but maybe I'm wrong about that. So much time has passed and so much violence happened between us that I could easily forget a smile on the night he gave me the ring.

I answered, "Yes, Charles," and that was it. Claire called Maman and we set a date in late April.

After that, little changed. Claire continued to stay in the bedroom across from me, though I noticed that both she and Charles became more devoted to furnishing her apartment so that she could leave. We still ate our long dinners. Charles now told more stories of his buying and selling, stories of deals won and, occasionally, deals lost. He went on and on, enjoying his own humor and drinking more of his rare wines than he had before. He brought fewer gifts, many delivered in store bags, not wrapped in ribbons, and these gifts began to hint at the life that was ahead. Velvet slippers, for example. A chiffon robe with see-through sleeves. Body lotions and powders. No more chocolates. I specifically remember that. No more bonbons.

Maman arrived a week before the wedding, giddy from traveling but not at my decision to marry a man she'd known all her life as singularly unattractive. She hugged me one hundred times that first night, shaking her head in wonder at what I had become in barely three months—a well-groomed young woman in expensive clothing engaged to marry an older man. "C'est trop, Mimi," she said again and again, not able to even articulate what was too much. Only that it was.

My maman's presence in New York, her exuberant heart and unmanicured hands, her coat that didn't quite fit and those sturdy boots, all gave me a start. I was forsaking her and the life we'd had, trading peeling wallpaper for silk draperies, and humble soups for steak done rare. I didn't want her life. I'd never wanted that life, had plotted always some grand escape. But Maman's life was safe and familiar and musical. I mean not just that she sang, which she did, but that the stories she told me rose and fell and her laughter had melody and the teapot whistled. I realized that, except for a chamber quartet concert Claire insisted I attend with her, I had heard no music since I'd been in New York. No singing. No teapot.

Claire's apartment was at last completed, so Maman and I stayed there with her those last days before the wedding. We shared a room because that is what we both wanted, and as she unpacked her borrowed bag, she hummed happily in

French. Do you think that is not possible—to hum in French? For Maman, it was possible.

She did not criticize my upcoming marriage. I knew she did not feel she could. Her own husband, if he was a husband, had left her pregnant in the middle of a war. She'd never heard from him again and after a few years, even forgot to tell his story. Still all week I'd catch her watching me, studying me actually, then breaking into a half-hearted grin when I noticed her. Once she shrugged some silent apology. I nodded and shrugged back. We all do what we do. We both knew that.

I threw myself into that week with Maman, dragged her up and down Fifth Avenue and into the park and to the zoo. We hopped on a bus together, something I'd never done, and traveled south then back, pointing at this and that. In her honor, I let my hair go wild again and if the day was chilly, I put on the old tweed coat I'd worn when I left Paris, though I never let Charles see me such. Maman and I walked to Times Square, stared together at the Broadway marquees, rode to the top of the Empire State Building. She held my hand whenever she could and I let her, those rough capable hands of hers, nicely shaped but always chapped.

Claire remained busy with her apartment, so most of that week I had Maman to myself. We spoke French. We ate sweets and compared them to those at home. I wish everyone I knew later could have seen me then, that week before I married Charles Bernard.

On our wedding day, Charles decided we would stay apart until the moment we met in the front of the church. As I said, he had not touched me before and so, when he lifted my veil, my face was as close to his as it had ever been. He nodded in approval and smiled with his lips together. Charles had smooth skin, almost hairless, I would say. And my proximity to that oddly smooth face struck me, somewhat repelled me, when he lifted my veil.

Together we faced the minister or priest, I cannot remember who they put there in front of us on that old stone altar with its white bouquets just so. We faced that man and repeated lines and said I do. Then Charles kissed me.

Even though I did not love Charles, I had believed that I would love kissing a man who emanated such danger and desire. But his kiss was tight and unsure. His kiss was amateur compared to those secondary school boys who had traded me small favors. I mean those boys were so hungry and wet and determined. I'd loved those kisses. I would remember those kisses long after I had forgotten who had kissed me when and where. Boys. They were so much fun for me. And I'd imagined Charles to be a grown-up version of that, mean and hungry and fierce. But he was not.

That is where the next kind of trouble began.

~ 3 ~

Hours later, alone in his room where everything was oversized and majestic, I slipped between the sheets of his bed and waited for Charles to make his appearance, his large sweep into the room, his fuss over the exact amount of light, his bit of a parade as he took off his long robe and revealed himself in silk pajamas. King Charles, I thought. King Charles of Manhattan.

Before the wedding kiss, I had felt challenged by Charles, like a boxer in the ring, fit and eager, dancing on my toes to make the first punch. Sexual hooks and jabs. But after our kiss on the altar, I was not so sure Charles was a worthy opponent. Those tight lips. That dry kiss. Then the royal sweep into the room. I watched him the way my maman and I had watched the creatures in the zoo just days before, curious to see what he would do next.

What he did next was hit me. He slapped my face hard and said, "You will never do anything I do not approve and you will never leave me. Do you understand?" Then he kissed me again in that flat way and pushed himself inside and came within minutes. He groped my breasts so that they hurt, which might have been my signal to fight back, as I'd imagined. But I did not. I held my breath and waited, and very quickly Charles seemed to tire of me. He got out of bed, strode like a warrior into his bathroom, and closed the door.

As soon as that door closed, I fled to the guest room where I'd slept those months when I first arrived and locked myself inside. I thought he would come after me, demand some type of compliance, but he did not. Even so, I never slept.

All of you with resplendent memories of your wedding night might think I should have left Charles right then. Who could be like Charles? Who wouldn't take time to encounter me beside him? Or even wrestle with my vehemence, my willingness to tackle and tumble about? Charles was a fluke of nature, the odd moss on the tree.

Maybe I could have traveled back to Paris with Maman and taken my chances that some other rich man would find me or I him. I still had options. I was so young and knew my powers, with men in particular. Certainly I did not need to proceed with this man who had no obvious instinct for pleasure. But I liked America and Fifth Avenue and I had my dreams of fame. Charles was a necessary inconvenience, a hardship like the other hardships I'd known in my almost eighteen years.

My construct went something like this: I would take acting lessons, I would audition for the American theater, for Broadway even, and I would find success within a few short years. When I did find success, I would leave Charles. I would buy my own apartment on Fifth Avenue, my own paintings and downy pillows. I would fly Maman to live with me. Introduce her to women who wanted fine dresses and loved hearing French. I would suffer with Charles only briefly. What was a slap, a bad kiss, a ridiculous man? This was my thinking.

~ 4 ~

When Charles arrived for breakfast the morning after our stark wedding night, he seated himself at the head of his table. "Would you like to take a drive today?" he asked, looking just past me.

Charles owned a sedan of some sort and employed a driver to take him wherever he wanted to go—his office, the train, the airport, an occasional, very occasional, restaurant. I did not know what kind of drive he was offering, and when I didn't answer, he shrugged and withdrew his offer.

"Another day," he said.

"I want to see Maman before she leaves."

"She's your mother, Corrine. Americans, even French Americans, do not say Maman."

"Because?"

"It is not American. It is old-fashioned. Like your mother's clothes. That's what you should do before your mother leaves. Buy her some clothes. And shoes. How could she wear boots to our wedding?"

My face began to sweat. "They were polished. She looked beautiful."

He snapped the newspaper up between us. "Go to Bergdorf's. Buy her everything. I don't even want to think what she wears for underwear."

I froze, fists clenched. "Charles!" I said this as a command, an order to look at me and listen to what I had to say.

He peered over the paper, amused at my authoritative tone, I suppose, or his own cleverness at provoking me.

"I will not buy my maman clothes. I love what she wears. In her homemade clothes, she has style that you will never know, have never known with your starched shirts and silk pajamas, cashmere stockings on your feet. Maman is mismatched and elegant. She is so—she is so happy. She hums, Charles. She sings."

He did not respond. He went back to reading his *World-Telegram*. And that night he uttered some new threat, I've lost track of them all, and hit me again and so it went.

Two days later Maman flew away to Paris. Like a beautiful bird, like a falcon on wing or a rock pigeon returning home. My maman. In America I never called her that again. In my mind, I always did and still do.

~ 5 ~

For a while after Maman returned to Paris, I avoided Claire. I just didn't want to see her or answer her questions or talk about how much fun we'd had when Maman was in New York. After Maman left, I began to walk the city on my own. As soon as Charles left in his sedan for wherever he was going that day, I would shake out my curls, put on my old boots, and start moving.

Don't ask me to describe the people in New York that spring of 1958. I didn't care. I cared about the city, the massive feel, the dark colors, narrow streets crossing wide, wide streets, the colorful cars, marquees and store signs, the dirty sidewalks and the way weather changed everything in a minute. I walked to claim New York and I did, I claimed it. I took large steps, almost marching, and dodged anyone in my way. Sometimes I threw my head back and laughed at the magnificent power of the city and the magnificent power I felt out on its streets. I learned to know the time roughly by the angle of the sun between the buildings. When I sensed late afternoon, I hurried home, changed into some sort of Fifth Avenue costume, and waited for Charles, so that we could sit in near silence at his dining room table and eat the many courses of food that his cook prepared day after day.

I didn't mind the silent meals. Charles bored me by then and my own thoughts have always been quite entertaining. As we ate I would think and plot and remember—all those wonderful things we do with our minds. All those busy beautiful things that need no one else. Charles would comment on the food. And we would say something about the world, the news. The French in Algiers interested him, I recall, as did Nixon's harassment by the Venezuelans on some tour he was taking of South America. Charles told me Alaska was to become the forty-ninth American state. "Who the hell wants that kind of place," he commented. "Eskimos and ice."

He had opinions like that all the time. I found them to be more amusing than anything else he said. He told me that an actor named Ronald Reagan had been excluded from a movie about the FBI because he had ties to Communism. Charles did not like Communists. He was all for making money and the privilege of wealth. The ruling class, as it were. Of course, he didn't live long enough to see Reagan-the-Communist become president of the country. Poor Charles.

Then Claire came by one morning as I was standing in the hallway waiting for the elevator. We surprised each other. "Corrine," she exclaimed with so much charm. "Where are you going in your old shoes?" She had quickly scanned me head to toe, her eyes jumpy despite her graciousness. "Has Charles gone to work?"

"He's gone and I'm going for a walk. Want to come?" She was wearing demure half heels, bows on the toes and all, so I knew she would turn me down.

"No, dear, but," she leaned close to me and reached for my hand, "how are you doing? With Charles."

I squeezed her hand and dropped it. "Well, we go our own ways until dinner. Then he tells me current events. I dream about jumping out the window and sprouting wings, and then we go to bed for some amateur exhibition or another."

She drew back astounded. "Corrine, my goodness. You've only been married a few weeks." Then her shock turned to dismay. "You're too young for this. I should have kept Charles in line on this. He could have waited a year or two. Given you time."

"For what?"

She fumbled, her poise not carrying her along as usual. "To grow," she said, but she didn't sound convincing.

I pressed the elevator button to open the door. "Don't worry, Claire. I'm old enough for Charles."

Of course, she didn't know what I meant. How could she know that my experiences with French schoolboys had taught me far more than her awkward brother's rendezvous with a prostitute now and then, for that was clearly where he'd picked up his limited and unemotional bedroom vocabulary. Though I suspected that I alone had unleashed his dominating cruelty.

Claire stared at me in shock. "I don't understand this kind of marriage," she said. She was wearing a perky yellow spring jacket and even that seemed to wilt with her dismay.

I shrugged. "What kind of marriage should we understand then? Maman's? Your maman's? Yours?" That last was an unfair taunt, I knew, but it was also part of the truth that enveloped our little circle, our strange little families. We had not known loving true marriages. We had known only varying forms of abandonment.

She took a deep breath. "What can I do for you, Corrine?"

I considered that. "Come to dinner more often," I said. Then I grinned. "Sure you don't want to walk?" The elevator had reached the lobby and I held the door for my maman's refined friend to walk in ladylike steps before me.

"It would be better if Charles didn't see you dressed like that, I think," she said, looking down at my boots as she passed out of the elevator.

"I know, Auntie Claire," I replied. Then I disappeared into the city on my own.

~ 6 ~

I returned to the theater district almost every day, trying to figure out how I could get from the streets outside to the stages within. My walking became more like meandering, lingering near the back doors of these theaters looking for notices, audition schedules, anything that might get me inside, and wanderings into theater supply shops to see what they sold and to watch who came and went. One day I bought myself a redheaded wig just to start a conversation with the blowsy lady behind the counter. "So how do people get into the theater in New York?" I asked, setting the wig on the counter.

"Whatever way they can," she answered, her concentration divided between her cigarette in the ashtray next to her and the cash register buttons.

"Are there schools or classes people take?"

"They got classes everywhere, honey." She looked me over. "You got a few bucks, they got a few classes."

"Who? Who runs classes?"

The balding, heavily made-up clerk leaned across the counter. "Forget about acting. It's the false parade of lonely girls." Then, like magic, she caught sight of the ridiculous diamond Charles had given me. She slid onto a gray stool behind the counter and lit another cigarette. "You want one?"

I took a cigarette out of the pack she handed me and let her light it. After a ponderous exhale, she said, "The hot shots go to a place called Actors Studio. Russian. In the moment, they say. Large moods and deep thinking. The best and the brightest. But—" she interrupted me with a wave of her cigarette before I could even ask a question, "nobody gets in." She smoked silently and stared off to the corner of the store where floor-to-ceiling shelves held boxes of mustaches and hats, wigs in all styles and colors, crowns and swords and every imaginable theatrical prop. "So what you do," she went on, "you go see this guy." She rustled around in the mess on the counter and thrust a business card at me. "He gets you ready to audition at this Actors Studio. Gets you in the groove." She wagged the business card without letting go of it. "You tell him Lana sent you. You tell him I said to give you his *best*. Wear that wig," she added with a husky laugh that sounded like she'd been smoking those cigarettes since she was five.

"I'm French," I said to her, eyes level.

"Good, honey. That's what New York needs. One more French actress with a diamond ring." She laughed her dark laugh again.

"The French are not fools," I said and slid the business card back across the counter. "But thank you for the thought. *Merci beaucoup*, as we like to say." I walked toward the door, then stopped and went back. I set the bag with the wig in front of her. "You keep this," I said. "Put it on and see how it feels to have hair."

The next day I went to one of her competitors down the block and asked about acting classes. I left my ring at home.

~ 7 ~

On one account, Bald Lana was correct. I found acting classes everywhere in New York, in church basements and rickety walk-ups, at NYU and Columbia, in the Village and midtown and in the schoolhouses of Harlem. And, in general, it turns out to matter little to my story because I didn't have time to develop and I didn't become a famous actress with my name on the marquee as I had imagined. No, I should not say as I imagined. I should say, as I believed. Even against the odds, I believed.

By the end of my first summer in America I had realized that singing and dancing were almost as critical for fame as deeply felt expression. Girls in my classes told me stories of notes they were not able to hit and razzmatazz steps they hadn't caught onto fast enough to get the part. In case you think I did not understand the real challenge, I did. I was not a singer like Maman and had never danced any kind of dance ever. So I understood. But I was just eighteen then and attractive and unusual and rich. I believed I would be the exception.

Charles, however, reared up at me before I'd even learned all the stage terms. On a steamy afternoon in late August, I came home to the apartment from a sweaty class in stage movement, my hair undone, my boots on, and wearing a handmade dress from my school days. And there was Charles to meet me as the elevator doors opened.

He didn't ask where I'd been or raise his voice or raise his eyebrows as he often did when disapproving of my very existence. This time he surprised me by striking me on the side of the head so hard that I fell over onto the thick carpet, too dazed to fight back. Then he yanked me up, pulled me into the apartment, and ripped off my dress. "Give me those boots," he said, much as the executioner might have asked Marie Antoinette to lower her head. He wrapped my boots in my dress, took them to our garbage chute and dropped them down. Then he stormed into his room and closed the door.

I retreated to the guest room that I had claimed as my own, and for the first and only time in my marriage to Charles Bernard, I wept. Not because he had hit me and torn away my dress, but because I'd worn those boots since I was fifteen. I'd worn them on all the narrow streets of Paris and on my escapades with schoolboys and on the airplane that had glided over New York harbor just months before. Maman bought me those boots, and not only were they mine, they were—as Charles well knew—me. Those boots were me.

That night I did not appear for the many-course dinner and I did not go to Charles's bedroom. I wondered if he would pound on my door, but he did not. Locked in my room, I slept long and well, and the next morning I went out to buy another pair of boots.

You are thinking, what was the matter with this girl? Her godmother would have taken her in. She, meaning I, would have found work and love and some sweet American life on her own. I know that is what you are thinking and it is a possibility I have returned to not some few times in my hard life. But Charles drew me to him in a way I cannot explain.

Ask the bullfighter why he bothers with the bull. One of them will lose, after all. Either the bull or the matador will lose every time. Yet the fighter will come again and again. He will swirl the full fabric of his cape and taunt and draw away and taunt some more. Because it is in his blood. The challenge and the fear and the desire to win are all in his blood. As they were in mine.

That rich awful man, I'd think to myself. That monstrous fussy bully. Let me at him. Once more and once more and again until I am the victor. Maybe Charles felt the same way about me.

Over the course of our marriage Charles hit me on my face and across my back, he threw me down, twisted my arm, broke my thumb once, pinched me, gave me black eyes, rammed his gilded figurines into my stomach, and dug his knuckles into me any way he could. In return, I never yelled or cried—and rarely flinched. I was heroic, I truly was. The reason I was so stoic and resolute was because I always knew I would win. Each offense only moved me closer to that ultimate end.

I didn't want some sweet American life nearly as much as I wanted to be the one who walked out of the bullring alive. I didn't consider the implications or the perceived insanity in all of this. I only knew that Charles Bernard was my opponent in life and, one way or another, he was bound to lose.

~ 8 ~

The next evening Claire came to dinner, chirpy and pretty, pretending that she suspected no trouble between her brother and his odd little wife. She hugged me in her delicate way, barely touching, her kisses more in air than on my cheeks. "Charles," she fluttered, "doesn't Corrine look lovely? How New York and marriage are so good for her, *non?*" She settled into one of the silk-covered chairs.

Charles made a sort of growling sound low in his throat and poured her a small glass of whiskey. "Corrine wants to be an actress," he said to his sister, paying no attention to me sitting across the vast room in another silk-covered chair. "She wears boots and rolls on floors to say she is something, what? A pebble on the beach, a tree that grows on mountains, maybe you are the moon, eh, Corrine?" He gestured upward mockingly.

Claire gave me a puzzled glance, and I laughed. "A great actress can pretend to be anything, Charles," I said, "and the audience believes her." I got up and poured my own glass of whiskey. "Even a tree, Charles," I said and turned to him. "Even a wife," I added and laughed again.

Claire's eyes roamed the room to find some salvation. "Well," she offered at last, recrossing her legs at the ankles, "it is good to have interests, to learn as we go." She hurried along, "I have registered for a series of lectures at the Jewish Museum on the art of Chagall. Now tell me if that is not interesting?"

I could see that Charles had no idea who she was talking about. He gulped his drink and said, "You two keep yourselves amused. I meanwhile will continue to work."

"You like work, Charles," Claire replied. "You do so well at working."

He scoffed. "Men I know get things done. They have success because they do not think they can grow from the ground like a tree or care why some artist liked blue or red."

"You are just in a mood, Charles," Claire said. "Art and theater are important too."

He walked closer to her in the room. "For what, Claire? That is my question. Important for what?"

"Charles," she started to scold, but she hesitated and then did not finish her sentence.

That night I returned to Charles's bedroom to maintain our tenacious balance. He twisted my arm until he drew involuntary tears. "You will never leave me," he snarled as he had before. "Do you hear me, Corrine? Do you?"

I think Charles demanded me not to leave him because it would embarrass him in his world of dandy millionaires—that some French wisp could throw him over. He didn't care if I loved him, only that I maintained my part in his own particular theater. That idea amused me. Charles hated my theater, but there he was, ever performing in his own.

~ 9 ~

I wrote to Maman once a week the first year I was married to Charles. I told her of my classes in acting and voice and stage movement, in face makeup and improvisation. I wrote to Maman about the coffeehouses I discovered in Greenwich Village and my weekly adventures about the city, popping into a museum or library, sitting on church steps, figuring out the territory of Central Park.

I used Charles's account at Bergdorf's to buy the most remarkable clothes I could find, Dior dresses and Cardin suits with contoured skirts, only to sketch them in detail and send the drawings to Maman. I told her of the clattering subway rides and all the pastries I was finding, not just French patisserie, but Italian fritters and Chinese moon cakes, sweets I'd never known before.

In return, I got a weekly postcard from Paris with one or two lines of her affection, memories, or tidbits—the tabby cat she'd taken in, the new employee downstairs at the boulangerie, that sort of thing. I knew she was buying the cards from the vendors along the Seine, searching for the best images of everything we both loved in Paris. I saved them until I had to escape.

But all that comes later.

Just before Christmas my first year in New York, Maman sent me a postcard of Saint-Julien-le-Pauvre, the very old church near Notre Dame, which she'd always loved best because it had survived since the twelfth century, the only parish that had, and because it referenced the poor, which she had always been. On the back, she wrote that she had married a man named Hubert Ramus who ran the street sweeper in her neighborhood and was kind and lonesome after his poor wife had died so young. "It was nothing, Mimi. It was small, early on Saturday with no fuss and lunch at a bistro. Jolly laughs and now he's here. It's good, Mimi. Don't worry. *Je t'aime, mon bébé.*"

When I told Claire this news she came undone as I had never seen her before or after. "We could have been there, we could have—we could have—." She called out one regret after another in her anguish at not being at Maman's wedding to a street sweeper named Hubert Ramus. She cried and railed and dabbed at her eyes with her lace-trimmed handkerchief until it was an indistinguishable wad.

"She'll be happier," I consoled, whether I believed it or not. "She is not like you. My mother does not love to be alone. And I am gone."

Claire stopped crying. "You think I love to be alone?"

We were sitting in her small library, as she called it, off her formal living room near to her formal dining room. "You like space around you," I answered.

She looked at her undisturbed rooms and wiped her nose. "I suppose."

"Maman will be happier."

"We should have been there, my dear, and you know it."

"She didn't want to impose. Can't you just see her drinking merrily in some bistro to celebrate? That's all she wanted. No fuss."

Claire shook her head. "I'm sending a fabulous gift—and you do the same. Go spend my brother's money on your mother." This cheered her up and we each had a glass of sherry to toast Maman and her Hubert Ramus.

The next day I bought my mother a goose down duvet with a linen cover and had the gift shipped airmail delivery, all so costly that I had both the joy of pleasing my maman and the delight in spending Charles's money. I never spoke of Maman to Charles. Her modest life with a street sweeper wouldn't interest him and he would be sure to say something that would make me want to murder him, as he so often did. Which, in fact, is why I have this story to tell.

MEN

~ 1 ~

I replaced my beloved boots at an army surplus store in midtown. The young man who sold them to me did not belong there, but on a ship bound for the farthest shore or climbing Mount Everest. He stood tall and straight, perfectly proportioned and solid in his movements as he organized merchandise in the cluttered, dusty store. "Are you an actor?" I ventured. "You might be Odysseus." He reminded me of Odysseus. "Or maybe Banquo."

He laughed and it was a very good laugh, a full and deep laugh. "You have me cast," he answered, because I had guessed right that he was an actor, and like almost every theater person I knew then, he was working the odd job to keep himself alive awaiting his moment. Except this Odysseus had already had some moments—the chorus in *Carousel* before it closed, for example, and a role in *King Richard II*.

He had been in the navy and loved the sea, although he had grown up in Indianapolis, which had no sea, not even a major river, nor mountains, nor anything magnificent in its terrain, he said. He'd been to the Hawaiian Islands and seen volcanoes more than seventy million years old. He was like me, I decided, in his desire for a large life. And so I waited until he was done with work and we walked to his aunt's apartment on the Upper West Side, where he lived inexpensively and made himself useful to her at the same time. Every Thursday afternoon she took a cab to Saint Anthony Church in Little Italy to play canasta with her friends from the old neighborhood, and he had the apartment to himself.

For many months, I met Odysseus at his aunt's apartment on those Thursdays and traded lovely favors with him, the best I'd known, for he had a schoolboy's fervor with astonishingly grown-up finesse. He'd been places, and he possessed an actor's imagination and focus. Need I say more?

He always set the alarm clock by his bed to be sure I left before his aunt's cab came anywhere near Columbus Circle, and he always walked me as far as the park, then turned me loose to make my mysterious way home.

He didn't know my married name, or even that I was married, or where I lived, because nobody I met ever knew those things. But this man didn't ask either. He called me Mimi because I had confided that my mother called me Mimi, and he liked the sound, the soft lip, as opposed to the hard edge of Corrine. And I was taken with this man of mythological resemblances, I must admit. So I let him call me Mimi.

Our pattern was that I stopped by the surplus store every Wednesday to confirm our Thursday rendezvous. For many months, we kept to this and afterward I would walk back home across Central Park with a great deal of energy pulsing through me, as though I'd been charged with light from the gods, as though my lot had been miraculously recast.

By then it was somewhere in 1959. I'd been married more than a year, I'd been away from Maman for more than a year, and I was still so very far from my dream of fame and freedom. I didn't want Odysseus to see bruises and so I placated Charles in those months of Thursday meetings, I did his dance more readily to avoid visible bruises. Then one bright Wednesday in late winter, I came to the surplus store to find a wizened old man behind the counter. "Help you, Miss?"

I took in the entire store quickly. Nobody else was there.

However adroit Odysseus had been, he'd moved on and left me standing alone in the dusty surplus store. A year later I saw him in an Off-Broadway production of something called *Ernest in Love*, a takeoff on Wilder that worked for what it was. I didn't make myself known, but I did think he was a believable actor. Truly, truly believable.

~ 2 ~

I had come back to the arithmetic of underpants. Who gets what, stolen bonbons, and so on. Considering Odysseus's sudden abandonment and Charles's continual battering, I decided, albeit obliquely, to be more cautious. I had given away too much of myself for whatever sack of goodies I received in return. I was losing my touch. Even little Marcel in the cloakroom might get the better of me if I didn't return to my old self soon.

I wonder now, however, if we ever go back to our old selves—
or if we are, in fact, always our old selves. Have I ever faced
reality, or have I always lived in the corner of Maman's hovel,
wallpaper flowers flaking above me, pretending I am somewhere else or someone else or will be soon? It's been a lifelong
speculation, to be sure. I'd let Odysseus call me Mimi. I would
certainly not make that mistake again.

I appealed to men, not because I dressed well or put on the
airs of those women I'd observed in my childhood, those allur-
ing creatures I'd observed in my childhood with high shoes
and red lips, but because I knew how to match men, eye to
eye and quip for quip. I understood the independence and
inner direction that ruled them. I even understood Odysseus
leaving me behind. I'd known that kind of arithmetic for a
very long time.

For a couple of years after I stood alone in the surplus store,
I kept to one-of-a-kind assignations. No more regular dates,
looking forward, daydreaming. No. I enjoyed a jolly actor in
one of my classes, and the bartender at a place near Penn
Station where I went for lunch now and then, and a graduate
student who was viewing a Degas ballerina at the Metropolitan Museum one afternoon and a very darling baker who was
the most fun of them all.

I also continued my classes, auditioned several times, went to
plays, and watched great actresses in the movies. At that time,
I favored Joanne Woodward, who won an award for *Three
Faces of Eve*. I saw the movie over and over to understand her
technique, then went home to practice Eve White and Eve
Black. You can image how badly I portrayed Eve White. I just
could not make myself grovel convincingly. But Woodward

was brilliant. Elizabeth Taylor also appealed to me, especially in *Cat on a Hot Tin Roof*. She had my kind of ferity, I thought. And she had violet eyes.

I began to get restless. I hadn't believed fame would take so long or taunt me so elusively. The other actresses I met were all doing exactly what I was doing—attending classes and auditions, going to plays and movies—and behaving as if, as if, as if. They were not a club I wanted to frequent. I saw myself as more rare, more obviously destined. I thought about places where I might meet directors or producers, poets perhaps who knew writers, or musicians who knew agents. Anything. I was twenty years old. Where was my future?

Just then, that early winter of 1961, I met a happy-go-lucky showgirl named Billy Jo. We were both rifling through the stage makeup bins at that same store where I'd encountered the blowsy bald sales clerk years before. This Billy Jo was hard to resist, all big chat and gestures, wide red grin and painted nails. I doubted she could act anything other than what she was, but she seemed someone who might know people, who might cultivate all sorts of associates in her easy, unassuming way. So when she invited me to her Valentine's Day party the next week, I said I would come.

~ 3 ~

Billy Jo lived in a place not so different from Maman's in Paris. She had two rooms and a bath, a broken fireplace, all up two flights and down a dirty hallway. I walked into her party late to find the apartment crowded with noisy, dramatic types posing sideways for each other as they always did, dressed up in fancy clothes. I stood in the doorway wearing the oversized coat from my schoolgirl days and the lemon cashmere scarf Claire had given me as a gift, a second scarf for the February winds, and my work boots, of course. I did not fit into Billy Jo's gathering.

But she hurried to greet me and gushed all over about who was there, all nobodies in truth, and just as she was going on about all of that, a graceful dark-haired man came to stand next to her. He also was dressed for some other party, not Billy Jo's and not my ragtag party either, but something else. One look at this man in his woolen suit, refined and calm, and you knew he was all about something else.

She introduced him to me and I saw that I troubled him. He said, "I know you," frowning as he said this, disconcerted at the sight of me. But, of course, he could not have known me. I had never seen him before, for I surely would have remembered a man who looked like this. Billy Jo went on about where he came from. He was an Italian from a faraway part of America with many lakes, I remember, because I immediately saw those lakes in this man's eyes, the blue of a lake, the cool, bright blue of a lake in the afternoon. I had not known a blue-eyed Italian before. Billy Jo said that his sister was a singer.

I didn't stay with him to talk, for that is not what I have ever done. I bid him a polite good-bye, believing I would see him again, because, for one thing, he had a sister who might someday be famous and, then too, because his eyes were the color of many faraway lakes.

I ate Billy Jo's food and drank her punch and left before anyone could stop me. Charles was out of town for two nights, buying and selling things in some other locale, and so I made my way to Greenwich Village to listen to music. A skinny guy about my age often played at the Gaslight in those days, kind of wailing and telling his tall tales, a kindred spirit I used to think, making it up as he went along. He became famous after that, one of the best fame stories I know, and he still is famous. Some think he always will be, a modern Shakespeare, this Bob Dylan. But at that time, he was just an outsider like I was.

In the middle of the second act, Billy Jo and her blue-eyed Italian came in and pulled up chairs next to me, asking questions and making a small fuss that was difficult to ignore. I have always been too much a solo act for all that commotion. After a song or two, I slipped away.

Zigzagging my way home, I did not think about the man I'd just met, but about the Gaslight, which seemed to be drawing bigger and bigger audiences that might include the types of people I should know. I thought about how I could be known. Honestly, I was always thinking about how I could be known.

But I should have thought about Billy Jo's friend. At one point months later, he told me he'd seen me the very day he arrived in New York and had thought about me ever since. He certainly was to play a part in my life, and if I'd understood Giovanni Paulo better, he might have served me more in the year ahead.

But one event at a time.

~ 4 ~

Whatever Charles bought and sold, he traveled more often than he had when I first arrived from Paris. He did not tell me where he went and often didn't even say he would be gone. The cook did not come when Charles was gone. She would leave me notes directing me to the various scratch meals she'd left in the refrigerator. In this way, I calculated how many days I had to breathe deeply and roam the city as long and late as I pleased.

A week or two after Billy Jo's party, I called her on a whim to ask for her Italian friend's address. I planned to be out and about and was motivated, as ever, by my curiosity. So at nine that night I located the man's building and knocked on his door. I knew Billy Jo would have called him, eager to share the news that I'd asked for his address. He opened the door wearing a soft shirt, loosely tailored pants and boots much nicer than mine. I walked inside to an atmosphere of corner lighting, sweet tomatoes simmering, and a lamenting melody of lost love playing on the phonograph. A bottle of wine had been opened and a plant of deep purple violets placed in the center of a table as red as that on the French flag.

"Did you cook?" I stood in the room stunned that a man had fashioned this kind of life for himself. He had not made dinner for me, simmered that pot of sauce for me, because I'd only called Billy Jo one hour before. No. This blue-eyed Italian had made a modest feast for himself the way Maman would have done, the way poor poetic souls everywhere do, cooking simple food for hours and putting flowers on the table.

He asked me to eat with him, poured glasses of the kind of cheap wine that Maman's friends shared. The music went on. Frank Sinatra, he said. Did I like Frank Sinatra? I wonder if I even answered his question. His spaghetti tasted better to me than anything our cook made, if only because it was so plain and unexpected. I barely spoke. I ate and drank and marveled at this man's red table and purple flowers.

I did not fall in love. I never fall in love. But he moved me, this man with his cooking and low lights. He let me eat without asking me a million questions. And his phonograph crooner sang.

When I was done, I told him I'd like to stay with him. "Here?" he replied, as if I'd just said something extraordinary.

"You want me to," I answered, because he most definitely did, and so he followed me to his nicely made bed against the far wall of the room near a clunky radiator that gurgled as it battled the cold of night. I'd had the wine and an intoxicating dinner, and I went into a state of passion that had only a little to do with the man who had fed me and who now trailed along with me as I raced into the moment. His sheets smelled clean, like he'd bleached them and hung them outside to dry, as though I had a found a bed in a real home three stories above Thirty-Fourth and Lexington. And he was an enjoyable companion, not particularly adventurous, but strong and caring. Not an ardent schoolboy, but a man who was present in his own mysterious way.

I awoke before daylight, rolled carefully over him, and put on my clothes. The streets were dark, but the bustle continued anyway, as it always did. Around Seventieth, I decided to take a cab the rest of the way home, and as we sped up Madison Avenue, I noticed a spot of tomato sauce on the fold of my skirt. Gigi. The Italian called himself Gigi.

~ 5 ~

The next day Charles came home from his trip and informed me that I was to accompany him to a business dinner, which entailed purchasing a black dress, he said, and black shoes and getting my hair and nails fixed. I understood this was so that the thieving gentlemen in his buy-and-sell world would not know he'd married a near orphan who traipsed about town in a hand-me-down coat. I put up with these demands of his, I always did. I asked nothing of Charles, while he asked mountains of me. I was always trudging uphill for him. I bought the dress and shoes, had my nails painted red, and had my hair done in silly but glamorous waves.

All this took days, and when the event was over Charles left again with his "colleague," as he called a man named Ivan, another European import. Ivan stood barely five feet tall and looked like he went out of his way to step on small creatures. Charles danced around this Ivan, clearly not wanting to be one of the flattened. At their highfalutin business event, Ivan studied me without blinking for so long even I felt uncomfortable. "You are Mrs. Bernard?"

I refused to blink either. "I am."

"Charles chooses a pretty wife then. Lucky Charles." His disdainful glance told me that to him *pretty* told lies, stole money, had affairs with more attractive men. In Ivan's book, *pretty* was anything but lucky.

"You have met my wife," Charles interrupted, proud of my hairdo and painted nails. "She is very bright, my wife," he added. "Reads books." He smiled at this great accomplishment and so did I. "A literate wife, you see."

"I do see," Ivan answered and let it go at that.

After Charles left on his trip with Ivan, I walked over to Columbia University and joined an improvisational group, more theater wannabes, largely ragtag like I was, but smart and funny, rolling around on the floor, as Charles believed theater people did. We'd pretend to be any number of natural phenomena and creatures. We played against one another, mimicked and mirrored one another, all with a certain solemn reflection that indicated our strong desire to be actors and actresses. Then we went back to our other lives. I doubted any of them ever went back to a life like my own.

This group occupied my time that late winter of 1961. I did not forget about Gigi Paulo. But I thought of him as another adventure that had come and gone. My rigor on sweet exchanges, bags of goodies and all.

When Charles returned from his trip with Ivan, he was angry and edgy, striking out for the least thing. I skipped an entire week of classes and wanderings to keep watch at home, wearing my Bergdorf clothes all day and doing a Yes-Charles routine that took the full force of my acting prowess.

I asked Claire over for dinner almost every night, because Charles never hurt me when his sister was around, though her presence didn't keep him from his many critiques and subtle denigrations about my habits, my inexperience in the world, my acting ambitions, and so on. Sometimes I baited Charles, I must confess. But when he was quivering with rage like a live power line, I walked a wide berth.

But in that tense week, my strategy of walking a wide berth did not work. Claire had been there for dinner again on this particular night, then excused herself early. A late March storm had begun to rage and the winds were high. At the dinner table Charles was testy about my imperfect hair and about the cook's potatoes, which he thought lacked salt, and about something President Kennedy had been quoted saying that day in the news. He walked Claire to the door, I heard them waiting for the elevator, Charles complaining about how slow it always was, then the door chimed and he came back inside the apartment. I was standing at the window looking out across the park, watching the snow against the city lights, gusts swirling high above the street. I enjoyed that view. I always enjoyed that view.

Suddenly Charles rushed behind me, turned me quickly, and punched me in the face so hard my eyesight darkened to black. And just as it came back, just as the room returned in all its golden splendor, he hit me again, and when I fell to the floor, he kicked me on the side of my head with his imported, polished shoe. It was his worst show of violence toward me yet. I didn't call out, which I refused to do, but I didn't stand up either. I curled inward and waited.

Charles roared into his room and slammed drawers and his closet doors and his suitcase lid, all the while cursing the likes of a bastard like me thinking I was anything better than the insect I looked like curled on his expensive carpet. On and on he went, not caring that the cook heard him as she cleaned up in the kitchen or that I lay motionless under the living room windows.

He called for his driver. He slammed more doors, and finally, he stood above me and said, "Don't wait for me to come back." Then he went into the kitchen to release the cook until she heard further, and he left.

It had been nothing I said to Charles. Nothing specific I did other than being the person I always was, not necessarily likable I'll admit, but not asking to be liked either. I'd only wanted a roof over my head in New York City, while I prepared to be somebody in America. I had not provoked him that night. It was nothing I said.

I put on my old coat and my two comforting scarves and went out into the storm. I walked without thinking, the wind beating against me and the wet snow drenching me thoroughly. Without thought or plan I found myself at the door of Gigi Paulo, who greeted me with such alarm and worry I did whatever he wanted me to do. I removed my wet clothes, took a hot bath, ate his food, and drank almost an entire bottle of wine. The lights were low as they had been before and music was playing again, this time one of those very sad ladies I came to find he liked so well. The radiators pumped heat and snow covered the windows. I did not think. I fell asleep in his bed, not bothering to dream.

The next morning the snow had stopped, the sun had broken through and when Gigi asked me if I'd like to stay with him for a while, I decided I would—for a while. I dressed quickly, took a cab to the apartment on Fifth Avenue, packed a bag for myself, and returned to his apartment where he had coffee waiting and eggs ready to scramble. His violet captivated me. "How do you keep it blooming?" I asked him that morning and, of course, he gave me a long answer about indirect light and some watering technique. This man was very different. Blue eyes and purple violets. No wonder he interested me as he did.

~ 6 ~

I stayed for almost three weeks. My bruised eye and scratches healed slowly, so I stayed inside Gigi's small apartment imagining myself an exiled warrior hiding from my enemies. I was not far from wrong. Charles, I learned later, was having me followed. Not Charles per se, but Ivan, who did not trust pretty wives. I didn't know it then, didn't notice the car that had tailed my ride back to the apartment for my things and stayed parked along the street when I ran downstairs to the corner grocery. I lived out those days of healing listening to Gigi's sad songs, paging through magazines, and watching out the window as the March winds made way for the light greening of April.

I started to work on a play about a deposed queen, thinking that this would be something I could use in a theater class someday. I could tell Gigi found it presumptuous, but then the man was from a small town far away from Broadway and Forty-Sixth Street. It never came to anything, my play, for many reasons, but I think I was off to a good start on it. I could picture exactly the way the queen walked and how she glanced sideways at anything she disbelieved.

Somewhere in those days at Gigi's, his sister showed up to use his deep old bathtub. I remembered that she was a singer, that she might know people who knew people, and so I reached out to her. I demonstrated my acting ability, dragging myself across Gigi's apartment as though I were dying on the desert sands, and she seemed impressed. Gigi's sister looked like him, though without his startling eyes, and she loved to talk. Gigi told me that all his sisters loved to talk. That is why he tended to the quiet, to hours spent repairing jewelry in the corner of a serene store.

The two of them took me to eat at a bistro, which brought Maman close to me and reminded me of what I had left behind in Paris. The food at the bistro was rich and the waiter spoke beautiful French and the room was tiny and familiar. I shared none of this. Gigi and his sister Isabella had their own history, their own stories. I wasn't any more a part of theirs than they were of mine.

Moreover, Isabella did not seem to know anyone who could help me in show business. She'd already been in New York for almost a decade, yet had not made a name for herself. No matter how many other starving singers regaled her, she was still selling hats at Bonwit's.

The next morning, after Gigi left for the jewelry store, I called Claire. Call it intuition. Or a bit of longing after my French meal, perhaps. "Corrine?" She sounded concerned. "Where have you been, dear girl?"

"Just staying with a friend, Claire. Charles left for a long stretch, you know."

"I did not know, my dear, because neither of you told me. I walked home from your apartment in that horrid storm and didn't hear from either of you again until today." She sounded irritated with both of us, but then her tone softened to say, "I found the locket with your picture in it this week. Remember that lovely piece from years ago? So charming, Corrine. You were such a charming child." I was not, of course, but I knew she preferred to think of me that way. "The clasp was broken, so I brought it to be repaired. I think I'd like to wear it again. You know I bought it so that I could claim my godchild, keep your picture close to my heart. Did you know that?" Claire could always get lost in the details of a lovely thing, whether it was a cashmere scarf, a locket, or a cup of rare tea. She never had to worry about the dangers of life. Her lot had been cast in the sun, you see. She didn't need to give trouble much thought.

"Charles called today too," Claire went on. "He's been in some other country, I don't remember if he said. But he'll be back in three days. He asked me to contact the cook for him and get the household rolling again."

"Did he ask about me?"

"Charles? No, he didn't. I assumed he knew what you were doing."

"He might not like that I stayed with a friend, Auntie Claire. It might be better not to say."

"But of course, my dear. It is a big apartment to be there all alone. You could have stayed with me, you know."

"I'm too difficult," I responded, which was true.

"Well," she laughed her sweetest laugh. What else could she do?

When Gigi returned from work, I went out of my way to mesmerize him. I acted out the part of a seductress, a movie star siren like Rita Hayworth, parading about with nothing on but my beautiful scarves. I was used to him by then and comfortable that he would love me without abuse or aggression. He told me I was perfect that night. I still remember it. But I wasn't and he knew I wasn't. I was not the only one who told lies, you see.

As soon as Gigi went to work Monday morning, I packed my things, careful to leave no trace, and left his apartment with its pretty little plant. I did not write him a note of explanation because there was no acceptable explanation. To Gigi I was a French waif trying to make my way in the theater. I had no relations, no connections, not even a decent-looking coat to wear when it was cold. He knew nothing, and I didn't want him to. I wanted him to imagine me. I wanted the violet on his table to continue growing. I wanted Gigi and his flowers just there where they belonged.

~ 7 ~

I did not get home ahead of Charles. He had dropped off his things and gone out again, giving me time to groom myself appropriately and brace myself for what might come. The cook was back in the kitchen. An April day blossomed in the park. And Claire arrived before Charles returned.

Our dinner reunion was awkward. Claire did most of the talking, focusing on that locket she'd rediscovered and art she'd seen at the Frick, where she'd also met a woman from Paris, such a lovely conversation they'd had, all things lovely for Claire. Charles pointedly asked me what I'd managed to eat with the cook gone all those days. I didn't know that I'd been followed, so I answered as if it were just another of his lofty inquiries.

"New York has so many restaurants, Charles, and coffee shops. On every block, if you notice."

"Why would I notice coffee shops, Corrine?"

Claire jumped in to save the moment, but Charles and I still looked only at each other, and Charles interrupted her to say, "What happened to your eye, Corrine? Did you bump into a wall?" He mocked the word *wall* in his question.

Claire then turned to study my face too. "Is that a bruise, dear?" My eye had healed to a faint bluish mark along my cheekbone, not prominent enough for her to have noticed until Charles drew her attention to it.

In answer, I repeated what Charles had just said—that I'd bumped into a wall one night, and I too emphasized the word *wall* so that she'd realize that I was lying. She glanced between us with concern. "Be careful then, dear," she said and lowered her eyes to her plate.

"My wife is never careful, Claire," Charles countered. "We both know that." He gave a false laugh. "If she were careful, she would never have married me, right, Corrine? An older man who gives you everything? Poor Corrine."

We all poked along through our pudding-like dessert and Claire kissed us both with great ceremony and left still looking worried. As soon as she was gone, I retreated to the guest room where I'd spent most of my nights in the three years with Charles. I locked the door quietly, not wanting him to hear or be on alert.

An hour later he knocked on my door. "The cook has left now," he announced, as though this were my signal to reappear. But I said nothing. I pretended I did not hear my violent husband rapping at my chamber door. Acting skills are useful in many situations, and after a few moments he went back to his room.

Charles did not travel for many weeks after that. All of May passed and the flowers of late spring bloomed, one color after another. Maman would have known what they were, but to me they were simply a medley, a sign that another season had begun and I was still married and still unknown. I returned to my classes. Sometimes I worked on my script of the exiled queen, who more and more resembled me on a good day. I won't say I never thought of Gigi Paulo and his sauces simmering, but not often and not uncomfortably. I mean, I didn't pine. I never pined.

I did, however, continue to meet men. I popped into a coffee shop one late afternoon and found myself sitting at the counter next to a very young man with so much blond hair draping across his face, that I could barely see his eyes. He put five lumps of sugar in his coffee, and I commented on this.

He was eighteen, just about to graduate from a private high school around the corner and was bemoaning his well-heeled destiny. What to do next, college or travel, credentials or experience, what, what, what? I advised travel and adventure. "Is that what you are doing?" the boy asked, and I said it was exactly what I was doing. I was informing my art of acting by living multiple lives at one time. He liked this immensely and laughed. He pulled out a package of some imported cigarettes to share and after we'd smoked several and finished many cups of coffee, the ardent schoolboy invited me to spend the next afternoon at his aunt's townhouse a few blocks from Charles's apartment. Auntie was off to visit a friend in Boston for the week and my new friend had a key. It was convenient and important, because this boy, Bobby Lane, would also be part of my story for many years to come.

But, as I said before, one event at a time.

~ 8 ~

Claire invited me to have lunch with her so that she could show me her trinkets. She'd found a charm bracelet that she'd worn as a child, though many of the charms had detached from the bracelet after years of childhood wear. She also showed me a garnet-adorned barrette that she said her father had given her for her tenth birthday. Then she reached underneath her silky summer blouse to bring out the locket she'd saved all those years, the one with the photo of me inside. I was maybe twelve or thirteen at the time the picture was taken, a time when I had so little and bargained mightily for that. I looked hungry and intense, I thought. Not like someone's charming godchild. More like a gamecock ready to strike. "That's not a very good picture of me, Claire," I remarked, ignoring her utter pleasure in the memento. "Do you think?"

"You've always been a serious girl. I accept that." She considered my photo for a minute or two. "It's you, Corrine." She smiled. "And I'm glad to have it fixed so I can wear it again." She dropped it back against her chest. "There's such a professional repairman at that little jewelry store near Eighty-First. This man can repair anything. I can tell that about him."

I recalled that Gigi worked at a jewelry store in my neighborhood. "Is he handsome, Auntie Claire?" I teased.

"I suppose he is, dear," she laughed lightly. "Nice blue eyes."

"Like many faraway lakes?" I responded, but either she didn't hear or my question did not register. "And he fixed that locket for you?"

"He did. Now I need to bring in the bracelet too. Thank heaven my barrette is intact. It's beautiful, isn't it? I remember how Charles sneered when I unwrapped it. What good is that, he said. He was so jealous." She laughed again.

But I had something else on my mind. "Did the repairman see the photo of me inside the locket?"

"The photo? Well, I wouldn't know, dear. Goodness."

But I knew. I knew that he'd seen my photo in Claire's locket, though it wouldn't have meant much or told him anything really. And now I knew where he worked.

~ 9 ~

It was just about that time, it's difficult after all these years to keep the chronology straight, but about then Charles became very social with the men from his club and Ivan's acquaintances, people who knew people, as he was always clear to point out. Many nights he did not come home for those extravagant, polite dinners with me. Charles seemed to be developing a night life of his own out there in the teeming city.

On one such night I was in the kitchen eating late when he slammed through the double doors, loving his own entrance, as ever. "I met a man who likes the theater girls," he said the instant he saw me standing at the counter. Then he lifted his eyebrows to emphasize what he had just announced. Some great meaning, I supposed. "Not the famous girls," he continued. "The rest. Your type." He laughed that flat, loud laugh I had come to know, without any humor or delight in it, the laugh of a villain about to tie you to the train tracks. And he went off to his room still laughing that way.

His comment had given me a start, a queer tingling in my fingers. I decided then that Charles knew about my life beyond him, that he had probably learned of my various trysts. He might know I'd stayed for weeks with Gigi Paulo. He might know where my schoolboy's auntie lived. Charles had something on me, whatever it was and whatever it meant.

The next morning, he waited for me to come out of my room. He blocked my doorway, shoved me against the wall and gripped both of my arms until his fingers and thumbs dug deep enough to cause searing pain. "You and your friends, you're not in my league," he said, digging in even deeper. "Do not take too many chances, Corrine. Be careful."

This was a recurring theme for Charles—this notion that I was reckless and the implicit threat that I would pay a price for it. But I did not think I was careless. I did not see it that way, and still do not. Even after everything that has happened in my life, I will never say I am reckless. I have always done what is my instinct, my nature, no different than the cat that dashes into traffic to kill a bird that swoops by in front of it. Maybe the cat will succeed and go back to nap in the sunshine. Or maybe it will be crushed by the wheels of a truck. Is that reckless? I do not think so. Our lots are cast. We do what we do.

A day or two later Charles left with word to the cook that he'd be back in a week.

I got a haircut that day at a fancy place nearby, then pulled a Fifth Avenue type outfit from my closet, a flowing skirt and soft sweater in the palest green. It was June, after all. And Charles would be gone for a week. Rummaging through my extensive wardrobe I also found a scarf to match my clothes and tied this in a bow under my chin, like a little French choirboy. I had this idea to celebrate a week without my awful husband lurking around corners. I had this idea to find Gigi Paulo again and see if his violet still bloomed.

~ 10 ~

The jewelry store was only a few blocks from our apartment, and I strolled there ready to enjoy my day. If Charles was having me followed, the damage had already been done.

What would it matter at that point? And too, I thought it possible that I'd get my theatrical breakthrough soon. I held to that, you see.

I stopped at the Hungarian bakery on Madison and bought a dozen kiffles full of sweet jams, then I went on to wait outside the jewelry store. I rarely compared New York to Paris, because they were so different to me, one old and winding and home, the other bold and busy all the time, a grid of numbered streets and tall buildings. But that day standing outside the jewelry store watching people and traffic pass me by, I saw some poetry to the city of New York in this well-heeled neighborhood where the pace slowed and a certain dignity prevailed. It made me miss Paris and my maman living upstairs of the boulangerie with her husband, Hubert.

When Gigi came out the door, he looked at me like he was seeing a wraith. "Nice tie," I remember saying, because it was bright blue and suited him so well. Still seemingly dazed at the sight of me, he told me that his sister had bought him the tie. "Nice sister," I said and offered him a cookie. A wind had kicked up in that hour, billowing my summer skirt and ruffling my hair.

"It's going to rain," Gigi said, worried, not sure what to do about the rain or me or the bag of cookies I was offering him.

"Let's go to that bistro where we ate with your sister." I longed for something French, some link to Maman and late spring days in Paris. We walked south down Madison, moving quickly as the rain began, first lightly and then with more force, a cool and fierce rain that made me happy. I loved the intensity and Gigi noticed that. He said I looked happy, and he seemed confused by that happiness. I was not the type to be happy, of course, he was right about that. But there are moments, aren't there? Even for the dark and hard-hearted?

Inside the bistro, all was as I remembered from our visit there those months before. The waiter bustled about us, the booth gave us privacy, and the menu was written in French. Immediately Gigi ordered wine and food and then he leaned across the table to ask, "Where have you been? Where did you go?" He wanted to know where I lived and how to reach me, "in case something happens," he said.

"What will happen?" I asked.

"I could get sick. I could have an emergency."

Dear man. There he was the picture of good health and robust youth, his tie knotted perfectly, his hair trimmed so neat, his life all in order. "You are well, Gigi. All is well with you."

"I am not well," he argued. "I don't even know your full name or where you live or how to find you. I am not well."

The waiter brought the bread, that crusty bread so reminiscent of my boulangerie, and I bit into it with such satisfaction. "Gigi," I said then, "you have a red table. Nobody is not well who has a red table."

"Why did you go?" he pressed, and that moment I made a decision. I pushed up the sleeves of my pretty pale green sweater to reveal the bruises left by Charles's grip.

"Who did that?" He searched my face and then to my amazement, he leaned even closer to me and whispered, "Charles

Bernard. He's your father, isn't he? He did this, didn't he?" I stared at him for a minute and then busied myself with the bread and butter. How on earth did he learn about Charles—or think he was my father, of all things? He'd somehow pieced together the picture of me in the locket and Claire prancing in and out of the jewelry store, but the connection to Charles? That I did not understand. I didn't want Gigi to think he could save me from Charles, who in fact would eat this gentle repairman alive in one simple swallow.

I dallied with the food, and finally I asked Gigi if everyone in his family sang. "Not all families sing, you know," I said.

Then to surprise me further, he whispered, "Marry me."

Again I concentrated on eating. I had ordered an omelette, the first I'd had since I left France, and I savored it as I considered what Gigi had just said. "Charles is not my father," I answered at last. When he pressed to know who Charles would be then, I told him Charles was Claire's brother, that Claire was my mother's longtime friend, that Charles had come to America and become rich and Claire had followed to "look after him."

"What do they matter to you?" Without knowing facts, Gigi understood that Charles and Claire Bernard were between the two of us. I had bruises, I came and went, my photo showed up in a locket and all because of my mysterious relationship with Charles and Claire Bernard. I felt sorry for him left to sort the likes of us.

"How is Charles rich?" he said, scratching about for something specific.

"He buys and sells things," I said. "He is probably a crook."

"And you all live together?"

I had to change this conversation. "I can stay with you, Gigi. Let's go to your apartment and I'll stay with you." I coaxed him away from Charles and Claire and back out to the gusty June storm that soaked us thoroughly. Back in his apartment I put my arms around him and moved him into my world, where questions did not have answers and the pounding rain blurred whatever was real.

The next morning Gigi declared that I should live with him forever, and I did not argue. I let him believe anything, because truly I did not think I would ever come back to stay with him again. I was a curse on the man. He cooked for me and we bantered about his ridiculously sad music and about the various sites in New York City where we each had or had not been. He told me he rode the Staten Island ferryboat at least twice a year just to be on the water. When I said I'd never been, we took an afternoon to do that. He skipped work for days. I lolled about in the patches of sun that dappled his apartment floor like an old cat with nothing better to do. I even wore his clothes.

On the day that turned out to be my last there, we talked about fame. I think I asked him what he aspired to, had he come to New York to be famous in some way as his sister and Billy Jo had. He found the idea funny, even preposterous. He said that his sister was not motivated by fame, but by the pure love of music. He thought that all his singers on the phonograph were motivated by the love of music. "They could sing in the shower then, Gigi. They don't have to try so hard." In his mind, I was missing the point.

"I want to be famous, Gigi," I told him. "I want what fame can bring, what it can do."

He laughed and remarked something about just wanting a good meal at the end of the day.

"Then we are different, Gigi. We are very, very different."

He was like Maman in his acceptance of ordinary life, of cheap wine and music in the background, of simple encounters and precise work done well just for the sake of doing well. He had no need to wander. He would gladly stay in his third-floor walk-up just as Maman stayed in hers. He thought we might get married and live this way together. He would make me meaty sauces and I would drape about looking lovely. We'd ride the ferryboat together, visit the bistro, have his sister over to watch a television movie. Or we'd move back to his faraway land of many lakes. Maybe he thought we'd do that. I suddenly could not wait to leave.

In the morning, I dressed before Gigi was out of bed. I tied my green bow around my waist just so and told him I needed to go, that I'd be back another time. But he knew I would not be back. He stood near his bright red table like a man abandoned on a lost island and with that vision of him, I closed the door and hurried down the stairs. A cab happened to be dropping off a businessman at the corner, so I slipped into the empty back seat and in less than a minute we were speeding up Park Avenue and away from Gigi Paulo.

MURDER

~ 1 ~

Charles returned late that same night. I had already gone to my room to read *La Dame aux Camilia* again, poor beautiful Marguerite, so wronged by the times she lived in. There are lessons in those classic novels, which I have claimed time and again: not to trust too readily, not to love too easily, always to exert your own intelligence and instincts. The writers of old knew something, you must admit. But because I did not expect Charles and had absorbed myself in Dumas, I was not prepared when he came into my room, threw my book to the floor, and buried my body with his own. I just was not prepared.

Who wants to know the sordid details of Charles Bernard pushing into his wife or how she pushed back to no avail? That story is as old as Marguerite's. Eventually he left my room and after locking my door, I sat in the bathtub for the rest of the night assessing my situation. I'd endured him for more than three years. His aggression toward me had never alleviated and now seemed sparked by whatever he'd learned of my independent life, the men and theater people, my wanderings about town in boots that disgraced him. I was a clever girl. I'd always known my arithmetic. But I must admit, I did not have a ready answer for subtracting Charles from my life.

The next morning, he said, "I am moving my office home for some time." He dabbed his mouth with the napkin. "So we will be here together, Corrine. I will be here to work and you will be here while I work. Maybe answer the door when people come to meet me. Look good. Look like a wife." He punctuated this statement with a decisive nod and a terrible smile.

I watched him finish his breakfast, bite by bite, his thick hands attempting to be refined, as he waited for me to rebel. But I did not rebel. Hatred moves in two directions, as you probably know—it erupts or it stows away. That summer morning in 1961, when Charles announced he intended to hold me in his sixth-floor gilded cage, I let my loathing run to the far reaches of my extremities and in every hidden crevice of my brain where it continued to pulse and pulse. That's what happened.

By midday he had a crew revamping the bedroom nearest to mine into his new office. He sat in a leather swivel chair and talked on the phone for hours, sometimes in English, but often in French, buying and selling across the globe, controlling his world and his money and me.

And so, as the heat of summer settled over New York City and kids splashed in fountains and ladies cooled their feet in the Central Park pond, I took up my life under Charles's watch. I spent long hours reading to escape my reality, sitting in the grand living room where Charles could see me nicely appointed, matching shoes and all, tidy hair. I devoured books like Marcel's sack of bonbons, whole series that allowed me to lose myself in the same characters moving through their adventures—Agatha Christie's Hercule Poirot and the Nero Wolfe mysteries, for example. I found Nero Wolfe particularly soothing, retreating to his orchids, never compromising, never beholding, devising complicated solutions to crime while his French cook stirred up airy soufflés.

Occasionally Claire would appeal to Charles on my behalf and we'd go out together, walk to the Russian Tea Room for lunch. She thought we'd encounter celebrities there, and maybe we did. But on those ventures away from Charles, I thought only of how I might escape, how I might excuse myself in all good manner, then slip out a kitchen exit, hail the first cab, and ride as far north as the driver would take me and on through Connecticut to Vermont and out of the country until I was gone, gone, gone. Who knows if we once saw Kirk Douglas eating gravlax at the Russian Tea Room, or Judy Garland or some other name of the era? I had other things on my mind.

I began to take small amounts of money, just in case. I'd ask Claire for a few dollars knowing she'd give me more than what I'd asked. I'd take money from Charles's account, telling him I planned to go shopping with his sister and hide most of it away. By August, I had five hundred dollars, and every time I left the apartment to spend an afternoon with Claire, I took it with me. I continually calculated how far I could go on that money.

~ 2 ~

My other life fell away. My theater classes went on without me, I supposed. Nobody, not even Billy Jo, knew my full name and so I heard nothing. When Charles sometimes left for a meeting outside the apartment—an hour here or there, no more—I called my prep school graduate, who told me long-winded dirty stories to make me laugh. He was only eighteen, after all, with few worries, and just that fact boosted my spirit, just knowing someone so young and free, so able to tell a dirty story like it was all that mattered. I hung up from those conversations somewhat elevated. Outside my chains the world bumped along, telling tales, laughing uproariously, tending orchids like Nero Wolfe, and daydreaming about what to do next.

I kept to Charles's plan, answered the door now and then to greet his absorbed and aloof associates. I ate when he wanted me to eat and wore what he wanted me to wear. But he never grasped the limitless nature of my independence. I was the girl who had run rampant along the narrow streets of Paris and wandered the many alleys of New York City. Charles could never own me no matter how hard he tried. I still had my imagination and my books and my plans for a different future.

Then the situation got worse.

One hot and humid afternoon in August, Claire arrived at our door for a visit. Charles was home, and I was half mad with pent-up energy. "You can't imagine, dear Corrine, how easily that nice-looking man at the jewelry store fixed my little bracelet." She had put it on her wrist, snug though it was, and dangled the childish charms before me. "I'm so pleased."

I had known that she would eventually go back to the jewelry store where Gigi worked, that this day would come when she'd bring him to mind again, tell me some delightful anecdote about her delightful repairman. Still her comment jolted me. While I had been pacing our apartment in restless frustration, Claire had been chatting about her bracelet with Gigi Paulo.

Hearing her voice, Charles came out of his office. "Are you showing off your trinkets again?" he said to her with his typical air of superiority, though it never seemed to goad her. I assumed this was because she did not feel he was superior at all. She had been favored by their father, after all, more loved and showered with gifts, such as the charm bracelet she jingled at him that afternoon.

"Of course, Charles, you remember when Papa gave it to me?" He frowned, thinking up some clever retort, I suspected, but then his phone rang in the room he used as an office and he left to answer it. At the same instant, the intercom phone that connected us to the lobby rang in the kitchen and I left to answer that.

"A Mr. Paulo is here to discuss a jewelry matter with Miss Bernard," our careful doorman said to me, his tone neutral, ever ready to do whatever the tenants wanted.

I understood in a second what had happened—Gigi had followed Claire to this building thinking he would find me. I instructed the doorman to send him up, then told Claire that the jewelry repairman was coming from the lobby to see her. Her face flushed girlishly, something I had never seen with Claire before. "My goodness," she fluttered. "This is certainly a surprise."

You are thinking why. What kind of trouble did I want to cause for Claire or Gigi or myself? I believe I wanted any kind of trouble, any kind of confusion or flirtation or even confrontation. Just anything to break the horrid monotony of my life under Charles's rule. So I sent Claire out into the foyer to greet Gigi at the elevator, and I sat in the most golden of our silk chairs to see what would happen.

Our large apartment doors closed behind Claire, and there was a brief pause, a suspenseful hush in the room as I waited. Then Charles slammed out of his office in that darkened mood I'd come to recognize whenever his buying and selling was not going well.

"Where's Claire?" he stormed.

"In the hallway talking with her jewelry repairman," I quipped with some amusement.

As soon as I said this, the fury in his eyes confirmed that Charles knew exactly who the jewelry repairman was in our lives. He flung open the front door and roared, "What is he doing here?"

Through the open door I could hear Claire say, "He fixed my bracelet, Charles. He's just stopping by."

"He's Corrine's lover," Charles blasted back at her.

"No, he is not," Claire answered, shocked and agitated. "You have gone too far, Charles."

Charles's voice dropped to say, "No, Claire. I have not gone far enough." He came into the living room and grabbed her pretty, pale blue purse that matched the dress she was wearing and took it back out to her, closing the door so firmly that I could no longer hear them. I rose slowly from my chair, smoothed my smooth hair, and walked to the door. Just as I opened it, Charles began to laugh, his head back and his voice angry, full of power and disdain. Claire had gone, leaving just the two men.

"Gigi is telling you something funny?" I asked Charles.

He spun around to face me. "No. I am telling him how we all will die."

Gigi, groomed and genteel as he always was, remained planted near the elevator. I was sure he had not moved since he'd greeted Claire on his arrival. Now I looked his way, met his familiar blue eyes. "You see, Gigi, how amusing is this little man I married, this little dictator man, so amusing. How are we all going to die, Charles?"

Charles growled at me and made some comment about killing me and how he would die because I was a whore, ridiculous in his rage, as ever. He parked himself in front of me like a small truck, though I ignored him.

Instead, I invited Gigi inside our apartment. "Would you like to come in, Gigi? Charles has a lovely apartment here. But no violet on the table," I warned. "No violets in prison."

By this time Charles had broken into a heavy sweat and his muscles were twitching. I knew what would happen. I knew it the way we know a gray rumbling cloud will bring a hard rain. He charged me, punched me in the stomach, hit me and hit me again. Then, surprisingly, gentle Gigi Paulo lunged at Charles and fought him to release Charles's grip on my throat. That gave me just the space I needed to roll away and thrust the high skinny heel of my shoe directly into Charles's neck.

As I broke away from the two men, I heard Charles moan in pain. I must say, this was a moment I relished, Charles in pain on the floor and me still standing. With blood dripping off my face, I reached for one of Charles's precious figurines, walked to where he lay on the carpet, and slammed the statue against his head with all the force still in me. Then I stepped back, cleaned my face with a blanket draped over the sofa, and pulled out my tidy hairdo to shake my curls.

~ 3 ~

Gigi looked at me, unharmed but agog. "Is he dead? Good lord, Corrine, did you kill him?"

"Of course not," I said, thinking that nothing short of a comet hitting Manhattan could kill the horrible man I married. "You are looking at a man with a very hard head, Gigi."

But, of course, he would not be appeased. "Does he have a concussion? We have to call a doctor, Corrine." His face clouded further, as though it were just occurring to him that if Charles were dead, it may somehow be his fault. "I just wanted to see you. I thought I'd follow Claire and find you. Now what have I done?" His eyes searched our gorgeous cluttered living room in desperation.

He really was too much.

I went over to him, placed my hands on his face to quiet his fervor, and said, "Gigi, you understand nothing. Charles and I hate each other. That's what we do, how we live. There's no reason to call a doctor, no concussion or sister Claire or dear Gigi with his sad music. This is me and Charles. We do what we do."

His eyes met mine in terror and confusion. "Why did you stay with me? Why did you come back to me?"

Gigi Paulo posed such questions that had no answers in my world. He came from a place of deep blue lakes. His sisters sang and his mother taught him to cook. He looked good always. He lived in an easier universe than the one I lived in. He did not want fame or adventure or risk or all the trouble that came along with them.

"You stay married because you hate each other?" he asked.

I had no answers. I shook my curls and asked him if he would like a whiskey. Then I went down the hall to my room to change out of my bloody clothes. From the back of my closet I pulled out a flowery dress that Maman had made me before I left Paris, a dress with an innocent rounded collar and tiny buttons made of painted wood. I thought Gigi would like it, and we would sit together drinking Charles's fine whiskey until the beast awakened. Changing clothes, I remember feeling quite pleased that Gigi had come by.

Days later I considered that while Charles had slept in some form of unconsciousness on the floor, I could have packed and run, taken my small wad of money and escaped as I had dreamed I might. But that afternoon in the sun-filled apartment, I felt almost content with my situation. I liked the big rooms. I liked Gigi waiting for a whiskey. The confrontation, on the whole, had enlivened me. I could knock down Charles if I had to, I realized. That is why I did not run away then. That is why I did not escape the sorry future awaiting me.

But when I returned refreshed to the living room, I found that Gigi had gone. He had not waited to say good-bye.

~ 4 ~

For the rest of the afternoon I sat in the various soft chairs of our living room drinking much whiskey and letting the light of the afternoon fade to shadow. I opened our windows facing Fifth Avenue to hear the reassuring sounds of the city below. I recited poetry to myself, rhyming "To A Louse" as I sat watch over the wounded Charles. *O wad some Power the giftie gie us, To see oursels as ithers see us—*

Even as the apartment grew dark, I remained on guard and he remained unconscious. Yet I was not worried. I had no worries that night, only a fleeting wistfulness that Gigi Paulo had not stayed to drink whiskey with me.

Somewhere well after midnight, Charles awoke and stumbled his way across the wide living room and down the hallway to his bedroom, panting and wheezing as he went. If he saw me sitting in the chair, he gave no indication and after I was certain he would not retaliate, I went to my own room and slept better than I had in weeks.

The next morning Charles left before I wandered out to the kitchen. Half expecting that he might be planning to attack me from around one of the many corners and crannies of our apartment, I glided silently from room to room to be sure I was safe. Then I made toast for myself and washed it down with just a tad more of Charles's whiskey, before I put the bottle back on the cocktail cart.

I called Claire to tell her that we were all alive and fine, that Gigi Paulo had gone home where he belonged and Charles was out conquering the business world again. But Claire was not fine. She had so little experience with the upsets of living, was so ill-prepared for enormous disappointment or miscalculation or anything that a soothing cup of imported tea or a pair of pastel shoes could not alleviate.

"Why did Charles say that about you and the repairman, Corrine? Where would he get such an idea? My word. You are married! You don't even own jewelry to take to the store, do you? I mean bracelets and the like?"

"Well, I have this oversized diamond Charles gave me," I retorted.

"Corrine, you are toying with me! Do you know him, Giovanni Paulo? How would you know him? What did Charles mean? I cannot understand this, what it means. Good heavens, Corrine. Your mother!"

"His sister is a singer," I explained, though I knew that this would tell her nothing really.

"You're not a singer. I've never heard you sing, Corrine."

KATHLEEN NOVAK   105

"Claire, I went to a party last winter with lots of actors and singers. Show business types that Gigi knows because his sister is a singer. He was there and he liked me and made me spaghetti. That's all there is to think about. I've never set foot in his store. I have no lockets or charm bracelets. I had no Papa to give me such things as you did." I stopped there, having shoved my own bad luck between us.

The telephone line went quiet. We both breathed and sighed and that is what went back and forth between us until Claire asked, "What happened?"

"You mean last night?"

"After I left," she said.

"Nothing, Claire. Charles asked Gigi to go and he did and we had a whiskey and went to bed."

"He did not leave."

"Of course he did."

"I waited outside. I sat on one of the benches across the street and waited for him to come out. At least fifteen minutes I waited and he didn't leave. I decided Charles had remembered his manners instead of bellowing at everyone in the hallway. So did Charles ask him inside? Is that what happened? Or did you ask him in? There was no scene then?"

She was pleading to hear a story she could believe, but would not send her onto a chaise lounge for a week. I knew this.

"He stayed awhile. Charles does not like him and did not want him here, of course. You see that your brother never lets me out of his sight."

"Go home, Corrine." Her voice came hushed and dramatic.

"You mean to Maman?" When she didn't answer, I said, "Maman has Hubert now, and I still have New York, Claire. In some way, I do. Don't worry."

"Mireille will never forgive me," she said in French.

"Nothing is your fault, Claire. I am not a fool."

"No, I think you are not, dear girl. But my brother is. And he is a bully too. It is not a good combination."

"Don't worry," I said again. But after we hung up, I knew what she said was true, that to have his way, Charles would stop at nothing.

~ 5 ~

I didn't want to run, didn't want to react to Charles, show him my hand or give him the satisfaction of knowing he had scared me off. I wanted to win. I still thought I could win. So that day after Gigi Paulo's ill-fated visit, I called my prep school graduate and asked him to meet me at the Central Park merry-go-round, one of his favorite places.

"You're out!" he cheered and handed me a swirl of pink cotton candy. Bobby was such a kid. Even years later when he was not a kid, he was always ready to ride the merry-go-round, so to speak.

"I need to get to auditions. I need to get out, to have a life."

"Kill the bastard," he teased and stuffed a wad of airy sugar into his mouth. "That's what I would do. Want me to do it for you?"

"Oh really? And how would a pampered boy like you do that?"

"Hire a pro."

"That's not a plan." I felt extremely serious that day. I had knocked Charles unconscious and he wasn't going to forget it or let it go unavenged. As I'd told Claire, I was not a fool. "How can I get out of that apartment to auditions?"

Bobby grinned. "Pretend you're sick and go to the doctor. My mom does this actually—sometimes daily, except for her it's real imagined not pretend imagined. Pick something chronic, like back pain or headaches—bad feet, maybe. Bunions or extra bones or something."

That made me laugh. You can understand why this rich silly person cheered me, why I let him follow me all over the world for so many years.

For an hour, we sat on a bench and watched toddlers ride the merry-go-round while we discussed potential chronic ailments that could get me out of the house several times a week. Bobby offered to search out the auditions for me—not him exactly, but his mom's personal assistant—and then arrange for his mother's driver to take me to where I needed to go. Bobby would drop off the week's schedule to Claire and Claire would give it to me without Charles's knowledge and then she would escort me out of the building to catch my ride.

"This is ridiculous," I said when we'd determined every detail of the orchestration.

"It is," he agreed and offered me his bag of peanuts. "You're like Rapunzel."

"Should we run away?" I asked this lightly, expecting lightness in return.

Instead my friend said, "Say the word, Corrine, and we're gone. Go be famous somewhere else." He stopped popping peanuts into his mouth and held my hand. "Say the word."

"I want to be famous here."

"Then kill the bastard."

~ 6 ~

Our elaborate plan came to nothing. I returned to the apartment to find a guard at the door and Charles's renewed determination to keep me entrapped. This guard, beefy and humorless, had been hired to accompany me everywhere I went outside of the apartment—even to Bergdorf's or the Russian Tea Room or Central Park Zoo. "Everywhere means everywhere," Charles clarified.

In response, I scheduled countless outings with Claire, traveling the length of Manhattan with her from a remote spice shop in Chinatown to a tailor on the edge of Harlem. I found a blind man who did massage near Columbia and a milliner from France in the Village. Claire and I ran my bodyguard ragged until Charles stopped us.

"You are draconian, Charles," Claire argued.

"Stay out of it," he replied. "Corrine and I know the game, Claire. You do not."

We were in the gilded living room standing amidst the many chairs and tables. Claire stared long at Charles and then at me. I did not defend our situation, because Charles was right. Nobody understood the dynamic between us, the fierce blood we were ready to spill just to survive beyond the other. But Charles and I had known this about ourselves the moment we met. It had started as a perverse attraction and had come now to this extreme struggle that Claire continued to witness. We knew one another to be ruthless and relentless and still we each believed that we would be the one to win.

Finally Claire buttoned her coat to the collar and pulled on her soft leather gloves with care. "Well then," she concluded. "I'm off." She trotted out the door in royal fashion and left the two of us to whatever game we were playing. She had her limits, kind and unsuspecting Claire did. If Charles and I wanted to behave so badly, she was going to politely excuse herself. Go back to her pastel rooms and write to Maman about the lovely leaves beginning to fall outside her windows. I did not see her again for many weeks. In fact, I did not see her again until the game had ended.

~ 7 ~

At this point the palette around me turned dark. The striking yellows of autumn faded to something brown and withered, as did the reds and the flaming pink of the maples. Inside the apartment, perpetually guarded and alone, I lost something, some reason or proportion. I forgot the hour or the day, forgot to eat or call Bobby or write any news to Maman. Like a tiger in its cage, I was out of my element, unable to lope or roam or hunt. That was me in November of 1961.

The cook was there every day, arriving late in the morning and staying until just after dinner, but Charles had threatened her too, so that even she gave me no relief, told me none of the stories she'd once told me of her children now grown or her long subway treks or how much she appreciated the whole chickens sent to us from a farm outside the city. All the casual nonsense of a normal person's life stopped. Even Charles's physical assaults stopped. Have you heard that abused rats live longer and better than those that are neglected? I believe this to be true.

One morning in this dark time, I heard Charles banging around in the kitchen looking for something—preserves or chocolate or who can say. He was rumpled, as though he had been up all night counting his money. His mouth fell into one of his standard sneers.

"What do you want?" he thundered, barely glancing my way, pitching tins of this and that out of the cupboards. I could see circles of sweat under his arms, more sweat on his chin and forehead. He'd forgotten to put on shoes or slippers, and I believe, thinking back, that his stockinged feet spurred me to action. I could still win. The man didn't even have shoes on.

It wasn't planned. I opened a drawer, took out a large knife, and the instant Charles turned from the cupboards to face me, I drove the knife into his stomach just above his belt and then—so quickly I did not know myself—I did it again and again. I looked at nothing but the red blotch growing on his white shirt and did it again. I don't know if Charles called out or flailed or showed pain. I felt only my hand on the knife and the strength I needed for the knife to penetrate and the hysteria that took over me like a dispassionate rage, a survival fury. I stabbed Charles until he fell onto the tiled floor. The floor was black and white. Charles wore black pants and a white shirt. The kitchen lights shone warm on all the white counters and through the windows I saw the gray morning clouds begin to lift.

I can never recall what I did next or the order of what I did next. I think for a short time I walked in and out of every room in our apartment, thinking they were all mine now, and also thinking none of it would ever be mine again. I rinsed the knife and my hands, but I didn't take great care. Hours later I noticed that blood remained under my fingernails. The body has something near a gallon and a half of blood working on its behalf. Once spilled, it cannot be poured back in. And so I had blood under my nails and Charles lay dead forever.

When the cook arrived, she took charge. She called Claire and the ambulance. She packed me a suitcase. Keeping the kitchen doors closed, she bustled like a woman who had dealt with death before, the administration in the aftermath, the organizing of what remained.

I went with Claire to her apartment. I don't remember that she cried. I do remember that she made me shower and put on one of her impossibly luxurious robes, and gave me her best tea. She returned me to the bedroom where I'd stayed with Maman before my wedding. Six framed prints of delicate birds hung in a straight row across one of the pale painted walls. I sat in a chair next to the bed for what seemed hours studying the sublime order of those birds.

~ 8 ~

By late afternoon the reality set in—Charles had lost. All his calculated treachery and all his random violence had not suc-ceeded. In those few minutes of my retaliatory rage, I had won. He lay dead. The king was dead. Long live the queen.

I called Bobby four times before I finally reached him. "He's dead," I whispered. "Charles. He's dead."

Bobby whistled long and low, as if I'd just told him I'd found a pot of gold. "I wondered why I hadn't heard from you in weeks. Is that why?"

"No. He wouldn't let me use the phone."

"So," he joked, "you finally killed him?"

"I stabbed him to death."

"Jesus, Corrine, don't go saying that out loud. I mean, this isn't—"

"I did," I reiterated. "It's done. It happened today. This morning."

"Where are you now, for god's sake?"

"I'm at Claire's."

"Don't talk to anyone. I'll have my mother's lawyer over in a jiffy. Jesus. Did he attack you or something?"

"He always attacked me."

"Exactly. So you just sit tight and don't talk to anyone. Not even Claire. Jesus. He was her brother." I think he repeated those same words again as he hung up.

I dressed and left the bedroom to find Claire sitting at her kitchen table, staring out the window. "He was all I had," she said without moving. "Mean as he was."

Nobody ever had more manners than Claire Bernard and nothing before in her life had so crashed into her reserve as this incident, this day when her godchild stabbed her brother to death. She'd done what she could do—invited me in, made the tea, contacted the authorities and the funeral home. "What do I tell the police when they come?" She looked directly at me.

I shrugged. "You know how it was between us. One of us was bound to die. Charles assumed it would be me. He thought he'd hit me just hard enough one day and that would be it."

"But it didn't happen that way," she answered.

"No. It did not."

"You can stay here, Corrine. I am responsible."

I never knew if she meant that she was responsible for my well-being or for her brother's death, because the doorbell rang and already, in less than thirty minutes, Bobby's mother's attorney arrived, a man whose presence instantly filled Claire's pastel living room with his power and efficiency.

"Lafayette Willson," he offered, stretching his hand out to Claire first and then me. "I have been retained by the Lane family as Mrs. Bernard's defense attorney."

"She's already accused?"

"No," the attorney replied with a terse smile. "But we will be ready if she is." He nodded toward me. "If you can get your things together and come with me, we will provide you a safe place to stay as your husband's death is investigated."

"She's perfectly safe here," Claire argued, and I saw immediately that she did not want to lose me on this day too.

"You are the victim's sister, are you not?"

Claire nodded with some hesitation.

Lafayette Willson raised one eyebrow, then looked again in my direction. "Please get your things."

I gathered my suitcase and reappeared to find Lafayette Willson talking with Claire about one of the paintings on her wall. "Mr. Willson appreciates portraiture, Corrine," Claire said, though her smile faltered when she saw my bag in hand.

"Thank you for the discussion," Lafayette Willson acknowledged politely.

As I buttoned my old Paris coat, I saw Claire's desolation. Then Willson opened the door for me and I stepped into the hall. I felt a terrible sorrow for Claire. It is the only feeling I remember.

~ 9 ~

I went to Bobby's guesthouse that afternoon, the police accused me of Charles's murder the next day, and within hours all the papers printed the sensational story of the businessman stabbed eight times in his kitchen. Claire put up my bail and a trial was set for a date in February. All that happened in a blink. It was my moment of fame, I suppose. Pictures of me made their way into several of the papers and I looked good. One of the images had been cropped out of my wedding photo. The photo editor must have concluded that I would draw more interest without Charles there at my side. Even so, it was one of the more unusual incidents in that very unusual time.

I spent hours in the Park Avenue offices of Lafayette Willson's firm. The details I revealed about my marriage—from my wedding night on—gave them great confidence in my defense. One of the younger attorneys sitting in on all the interviews developed such a pained expression, such shock and worry, that I had to quit looking his way.

But my sorry marriage had few witnesses, that was the problem. Or so Lafayette Willson contended. "Your husband was a successful businessman. The prosecution will parade no end of his colleagues out in support of his upright character and loyalty and so on. Battered wives do not tend to be believed," he said. "Unless you have proof or witnesses. Even then it is not an easy defense."

I regretted never taking my wounds to an emergency room. I regretted even my obstinate privacy. Claire had seen some of my bruises and knew her brother's malevolence ran deep. But he had never hit me in front of her. Only Gigi had seen Charles hit me. Only Gigi. I told the defense team of our living room scene three months before and gave them Gigi's name and where he worked. At the end of that same week, the team called me back in for a conference.

"Your friend Giovanni Paulo told us (a) you were more than friends, (b) you have lived intimately with him for brief stretches of time, and (c) that he has seen you initiate violence against your husband beyond self-defense." Lafayette Willson rattled this off with the speed of a machine gun. The man was something of an intellectual machine gun, actually. "We cannot use him. He's a stick of dynamite."

I listened dumbfounded. Of course, everything Gigi had told them was true. Black-and-white truth. But is that the only truth? No. Truth comes in layers like the *mille-feuille* we sold at my Paris boulangerie. Damn Gigi Paulo, believing in only one truth. I had a father, for example. Technically and in truth. But was he married to Maman? Did he fight for us and France or was he a ne'er-do-well who scurried off with the masses when Hitler's troops came near? I had lived my entire life in layers of truth. Was Charles Bernard even my husband? Technically and in truth? Given my age and his ridiculous behavior, I might have had it annulled the day it began.

"Gigi Paulo is mistaken," I replied to Lafayette Willson. "Young men in love can be mistaken." I sat rigid in their cushioned office chairs and stared with steel at the lot of them, righteous attorneys and their straitlaced assistants in tight skirts. I shook my hair wilder. "Now what?"

They had their glances all around, knowing, concerned, grave. They were, in general, a grave bunch. "We'll proceed without him," my brilliant lawyer said. "We'll make the best of it."

"The best of what?" I asked.

Willson took a deep breath before he said, "You are twenty years younger than your husband was. Your sister-in-law will testify to his temper and that she suspected he abused you and was always uncomfortable with the marriage. Your cook will testify to your husband's rages. One of your former acting instructors, seeing your picture in the news, contacted us to say he remembered seeing bruises. Another resident of your building came forth as well. She lives on the floor below you and saw you once with a black eye. So we have that." He nodded to himself absently, adding it up in his head to determine if it was enough.

It wasn't enough. I knew it wasn't enough.

But it was something. The fact of Claire testifying on my behalf encouraged me some, as did an acting instructor coming forward, whichever one, they hadn't said. And a neighbor as well. I recalled the round, corseted lady below us who wore feathers in her hats and reminded me always of Maman's clients—that terrific effort to match all parts together. These people would step forward and not Gigi.

That exact night of the intense conference on Park Avenue, Bobby and I went to a movie in midtown and afterward, out in the cold dark air, I saw Gigi walking home from work, his lean figure moving with the crowd, his beautiful face somber. And just as I spotted him, his eyes met mine, as if in all the enormous bustle of Manhattan before Christmas, there were only the two of us with our linked destinies that caused us both such trouble. Bobby whispered something outrageous then and I laughed in abandon. To hell with you, Gigi Paulo. I'll be free without your help.

I didn't shout that, of course. I laughed it on the December air. It felt so very good to laugh that way.

~ 10 ~

I spent the next months in Bobby's family guesthouse on the top floor of a grand prewar building. Bobby made sure I had what I needed and his mother's assistant, Beatrice by name, came by almost daily with a notebook where she scribbled reminders to herself. I did not want for anything.

Bobby Lane was my largest friend in life. He did not bore me as the school girls in Paris had or counter me so perfectly as Marguerite had. He displayed none of the serious intentions of Gigi Paulo and did not leave me as Odysseus had done. If Maman had had a son, he would have been Bobby

Lane, all buoyant and ready, constant and kind. Much kinder than I have ever been, certainly. So while he'd been my silly companion for some months before Charles died, he became my protector thereafter. Not just in the immediate aftermath, when I needed to sidestep the law and reestablish myself, but also later and later again.

Bobby never asked for anything but my attention and—on very long, quiet nights—the rollick of my favors. I always wondered how he could be that way, so lacking in self-interest, especially considering that he was an attractive man who might have named his future on many fronts rather than roving about with an outlaw like me. I have concluded it was because Bobby was born in the sun and there he remained. He was smart enough to do well in school and good looking and quick to catch the joke or the mood or the ball if someone threw it to him. He never scrapped. Never.

Let me tell you something else—old money is a thing apart. It goes deep like the roots of an ancient oak. It's a cushion of comfort unbeknownst to the likes of Charles Bernard or even Claire in her pastel rooms. My husband and his sister had money in an exact figure, a certain amount, albeit high, but not unlimited. Claire could live well for a century and not run out of money and she nearly did, as a fact, and had plenty left over when she was gone. But that was just Claire. It wasn't generations of offspring and their offspring, begats that go on for centuries all living well without worry.

Bobby told me his mother's great-grandfather had a hardware store when he was young, invested his money in banks and other financial institutions and also in an iron company. It went on from there, the money multiplying like rabbits, until there was no end to it, Bobby said.

We sat in his mother's guesthouse one night before the trial, lounging on fat chairs and contemplating the future. "What if I have to escape?" I asked him.

"I'll go with you."

"Where?"

"Anywhere, Corrine. Where do you want to go?"

"Far," I answered, Thursday's child that I was. "I might need papers, you know. I might need to be someone else."

He said yes, it could be done. He could get me a passport and smuggle me anywhere I wanted to go no matter how far. For Bobby Lane and his family's roots that ran to the center of civilization, anything could be done. I want to say for the record that at that point I hoped Lafayette Willson and his team were as shrewd as they portended to be and that the trial might still go my way. I wanted to move back to the apartment above Fifth Avenue and capitalize on my newfound fame. I imagined becoming a local figure, someone recognized on the streets and admired for my unorthodox life and bravery against a brutal man. Youth dreams, as they say.

EXILE

~ 1 ~

Would I say that I was nervous all those weeks awaiting my trial?

I may have been and I certainly should have been, but I will also say that I was prepared. I had youth and beauty on my side and the ability to act the role of a fragile, abused young wife who feared her violent and domineering husband. It was an interesting acting role—worthy of a Broadway drama. Joanne Woodward would have done well with it.

I found a motherly salesclerk at Bergdorf's to help me look the part, a Mrs. Goldbloom, who scolded, "Darling girl, you appear much too wild." She put on the glasses that dangled from her neck and studied me. "Of course you are innocent," she said at last. "That face, of course, that face is innocent. But not this coat. Not these boots." She shook her head in dismay. "You must be reserved, darling. Retiring. That's what I mean. Somber." Then she caught herself. "Not too somber. Not dark. We go with some white—white blouse, white collar, and blue, dark blue, but not too dark blue. Not bright blue. Not baby blue. No pink. Let's see." She flipped through racks of clothing and brought out one outfit after another, instructing me on how to wear them, which outfit needed a hat, what kind of hat, cuff links on the shirt, but not flashy cuff links, maybe pewter and so on. Mrs. Goldbloom should have won an Oscar.

Then to ensure that everything fit perfectly, she called out a tailor, a tiny lady with messy gray hair and a tape measure around her neck, who said nothing to me. She stuffed her mouth with pins and tugged on the skirts for me to turn and made throaty noises to demonstrate her reactions to what we were doing. Possibly, she didn't even know English. But in her hands, I felt back in a familiar country again, in a place where seamstresses scurried along the floor making tucks and folds and gathers and hems. I missed Maman.

When I left Bergdorf's that day, I called Claire. "Does my mother know what happened?"

"A newspaper found her."

This surprised me. "How do you know?"

"She called me, Corrine. She said some newspaper person, a Parisian I believe, came to the apartment and asked her if she was related to Corrine Bernard. And of course, dear Mireille said yes, yes, you were her daughter. So this vile person asked did she know her daughter had stabbed her husband to death with a kitchen knife. All of that, this reporter said. Kitchen knife, he said. Your mother chased the man away and called me, spending that money to call me. I told her to hang up and I called her back. We talked for some time."

"What did you say?"

"That Charles was cruel. It was an accident. You are a lovely girl." I heard Claire's breathing through the phone line.

"I am not a lovely girl. Maman knows I have never been a lovely girl."

"Still," Claire replied, "it is something to say. And I told her all would be fine. Nothing would come of it. Certainly your mother knows what a foolish bully Charles was." I have always admired Claire's loyalty to me at that time, her unwillingness to blame me for her brother's death, her belief that he had provoked me as he had provoked all her friends in Paris back when. She didn't enlarge my part in it all. In some way, she refused to accept it.

"You think I should call?"

"See what happens. How it goes. Maybe you will go home to her soon. When the news is good, then call her."

We hung up soon after. Claire did not ask me where I was staying, and I did not ask her what she was doing with our apartment. I did not even ask her about money, though over time she always made sure I had money. I think I did tell her about my serious outfits from Bergdorf's. That was the sort of thing she would have wanted to hear.

I took Claire's advice. I did not call Maman. And this is one of the regrets of my difficult life. I did not call Maman, I did not hear her lyrical voice, I did not assure her and listen to her coo dear Corrine, *ma chère*. I would wait until after I was acquitted. I would wait until I was free from everything that had to do with Charles, then I would return to visit Maman with a suitcase of gifts and great stories to tell. I would return to Maman and—despite her husband, Hubert—I would crawl into my bed under the eaves and stare again at that ancient flowered wallpaper.

~ 2 ~

The first week of my trial brought forth one grim detail after another—the number and depth of the stab wounds on Charles's body, the large and ominous kitchen knife, the coroner's report on what organs had been damaged and the actual cause of his death. Apparently I had hit some key artery in the stomach area. Or several. The testimonials went on and on. The medical people who had arrived with the ambulance and the police who followed them all had their stories to tell.

The prosecution even presented our cook, a hostile witness they said, because she didn't want to betray the "poor girl," as she called me again and again. Still, as an honest, hard-working woman, she did me considerable damage under oath. Yes, the couple were home alone that morning until she arrived and yes, Mr. Bernard was dead when she entered the kitchen and yes, blood had splattered everywhere which, without thinking, she had wiped clean with paper towels. And what had she done with those paper towels? She had tossed them into the garbage incinerator. And so on.

She looked at me often in her long questioning, regret in every muscle, and so I nodded her way. Not in reassurance, but in recognition. We do what we do, as I have said before.

Lafayette Willson worked hard in his cross-examination of the cook in an effort to change perceptions from the horror of blood all over the kitchen to sympathy for a young woman—a poor girl, as it were—who lived with a violent man. He asked the cook about Charles's temper and absences, his constant beratings and general unkindness. "He weren't nothing like his sister," she said at some point. Then Claire became the "poor woman" for the rest of the cook's testimony.

Every night I went back to the guest apartment, smoked an entire pack of cigarettes, and drank whiskey, which the Lane family provided. I wanted no company, talked to no one, not even Bobby who would have preferred to hover like a hummingbird. I needed to be alone. I stared out a window at the winter sky, mostly cloudless and cool, and I focused on my characterization. Who was I? Corrine Michel Bernard, abandoned daughter of a French soldier and wife of a ridiculous businessman who kissed with stiff lips and hit me in the face. I focused on that.

And every day in court I played my part. I sat still. I did not cross my legs or lean on the table. My hands stayed clasped in my lap and I kept my back straight. I wore no frivolous jewelry, certainly not my monstrously large wedding ring. I never smiled. I never frowned or showed feeling of any kind. I remained graceful, I believed, and reserved, as Mrs. Goldbloom had instructed. The newspapers described me as beautiful. A child bride.

On the first day in the courtroom, I turned at recess to see Billy Jo, the chatty showgirl who had introduced me to Gigi Paulo. She fluttered a wave, completely understanding the theatrics of the moment. I noticed that she came almost every day after. I also noticed that her happy wave faded over the days to a worried nod in my direction. Clearly she didn't think the trial was going my way.

Neither did I.

~ 3 ~

Lafayette Willson based his defense on hearsay and inference. That was all he had. The elderly neighbor in her feathered hat who had seen me with a black eye once as we rode the elevator together. The acting teacher, an aspiring actor himself, who sounded highly credible, but could say little of consequence since he never knew the circumstances of my bruises. Claire testified for me as well, loyal to Maman as she was. Although she had never seen Charles hurt me physically, she tried to be helpful. She looked, of course, proper and kind, her face sympathetic and worried, her voice so gentle.

Her brother had always had a temper, she said, and she'd been concerned about my welfare since the early days of our marriage. "She's a lovely child," Claire told the packed court-room. "I've known her all my life."

That evening I wondered if, in some peculiar way, Claire did think I was a lovely child. I thought it over for a long while as I smoked my cigarettes, gazing out the high windows at New York's night sky. In the end, I concluded that Claire possibly thought everyone at least a little bit lovely. She had no reason not to think that. She needed no enemies to arm herself against. Life came easily. Why shouldn't she love it and me and anyone who entered her universe?

Willson surfaced other important facts—that I would benefit from no life insurance, for example, and that Charles had had me followed for nearly a year, tracking my whereabouts on a daily basis. He recalled Ivan to the stand, who under oath, sneered that Charles had come to hate his wife. "And why wouldn't he?" Ivan ended.

But after just two days of my defense, I realized how much I needed Gigi to say what he'd seen and what he knew, and that without his testimony, I may actually be convicted. I came home at the end of that second day of my defense in a state. I put on my coat and boots and went out onto the streets to clear my mind and come up with some plan. But I was too rattled to think straight. Instead I found myself walking with fierce speed to Gigi Paulo's door and pounding on it so hard I hurt my hand.

He opened the door looking as he always did, serene and dreamy, handsome and self-possessed. "Are you going to ask me in?" I barked at him. "Or are you going to strand me out in the hallway?" At that he stepped aside and held the door for me. His lights were low, as ever, the violet continued to bloom on his table, and some husky African voice sang in the background. "Why did you tell my lawyer that we were lovers, Gigi?"

He drew back. "Because it's true."

"So what?" His simplicity exasperated me to near tears. "If I'm in prison for the rest of my life what good is that gorgeous truth of yours? You tell me!"

He had no answer to that.

"You know it was self-defense, Gigi. You saw Charles punch me in the face. I had bruises every time you saw me. That's truth too. You know it is, but you won't say. Why won't you say? Are you going to get me convicted of murder because I didn't leave Charles for you?" Saying these things made me more and more hysterical. "You could save me. Claire tried to save me and you won't. Why won't you?"

He stood mute across from me until I slammed my hands so hard on the red table top that he jumped.

"You could have left," he said suddenly.

I checked my emotions and said as reasonably as I could, "You can still save me, Gigi."

I stared at him, willed him to do as I wished, to show that he loved me, to save me as I needed him to. Instead he whispered, "You stabbed him eight times."

That number. Eight times. Eight stabs into King Charles. I said, "Maybe it took eight times."

"Why?" Gigi asked, groping for something—reason or belief or hope. Something.

He never understood, that was the problem. "Why what? Why get rid of Charles, why use a kitchen knife, why not run away with you to some thousands of lakes?" I was shouting again. "There are no whys, Gigi. There is only you refusing to help me." I turned and yanked open his door. "You could save me and you won't. My god, why won't you?" By then I was sobbing and completely out of control. The man's resolute face, his inability to grasp the full meaning of what he was doing to me were all so impossible for me to accept. I had thought Gigi Paulo would be willing to rescue me from anything—and now he couldn't rescue me from the largest horror. I ran down his stairs and continued at full pace for many blocks.

Then my breathing slowed to a near stop. I knew what I had to do and walked in hard, deliberate steps back to the guesthouse to make my preparations.

~ 4 ~

Mrs. Goldbloom's tour de force on my behalf was a navy blue, wool crepe dress, dark but not too dark, as she said, that floated over me like gossamer. She'd matched this prize with navy suede pumps and a softly veiled hat. Think delicate, aggrieved wife. Reviewing how well I presented and how sensational my marriage, I have reflected that Lafayette Willson made a mistake in not calling me to the stand. Even before the trial, I wondered that.

Bobby said it was because Willson sensed "an element of unpredictability" in me.

"What the hell does that mean? Who knows my wretched story better than I do?"

Bobby had fidgeted. "He may not want to risk it."

"Risk what? Does he think I'll suddenly explode into expletives?" Bobby did not answer. He lit another cigarette. "You already have one in the ashtray," I pointed out.

"Just let Willson do his job."

So I did. But there in the second week of the trial, amidst the limping testimonies of witnesses who knew only half of my reality and whose credibility was almost immediately blown away by the prosecuting attorney, I wished to be on the stand defending myself. And on that day of the navy dress, I think nobody would have failed to think me innocent. Victimized. Even righteous.

But the testimonies staggered along—the doorman at our building, Claire recalled for one more nicety. I sat so retiring that Mrs. Goldbloom would have surely beamed in complicit approval.

At the noon recess, I excused myself from Lafayette Willson's watch to use the courthouse bathroom, as I had done every day of the trial. The veil on my hat covered half of my face. Mrs. Goldbloom thought it made me look solemn, even virtuous. And as I said, it covered half of my face. I was still recognizable, I suppose. The young woman who had stabbed her husband until he fell in a heap to the floor.

During lunchtime, the courthouse teemed with activity. Rivers of dark-suited attorneys and their staffs flowed in every direction, doors opening and closing, impromptu clusters talking intensely. I counted on this fervor the way the rabbit counts on the evening light. For I was about to disappear. I was about to transform from the wife on trial to a free agent of the universe. I turned and strode out fast, walking without even a glance in any direction but the door, through the dark suits, eyes straight ahead until I was outside in the biting February air, where I slid into the waiting car and—before my back even rested against the car seat—was zipped off and speeding through the city.

If perchance someone had called out or wanted to deter me, I would have found another opportunity soon, another magic act that erased the presence of Corrine Bernard. At that point, it was inevitable. It was, as Maman often said of her life in Paris, *mon destin.*

Even so, I knew I could have been foiled in countless ways. I've considered this so often through the years. In the long hours of that night after my last plea to Gigi, Bobby had orchestrated my flight, the driver, the identity, the small house at the end of an island, and not just all that, but the next move and the next. That is what I mean about old money. Doors open wide enough for a whole person to slip away into another locale, another state, another country. I didn't see Bobby for some time. He'd arranged a series of "handlers" to pass me along, bring me supplies, and guard me.

At the far end of Long Island, I held up in a remote cottage where I camouflaged myself as appropriate. Bleached my hair and chopped it short, crazy white curls in every direction. I looked like a clown at that phase, let me tell you. Claire would have been aghast. For that interim I was renamed Michelle Rhodes—Michelle because it was similar to Michel and Rhodes because it was a synonym for Bobby's surname, Lane. It was all quite silly, when I look back. Very cloak and dagger, very *Count of Monte Cristo.* But it did allow me a new passport and that was not silly at all.

While the newspapers reported a series of outlandish rumors— even that Gigi Paulo was involved in my disappearance—I walked the bare winter beaches of the Atlantic and thought more and more of what now would not be. I would not be a famous actress in New York. I would not live six stories above Fifth Avenue with my view out to the park. Or wander the streets in adventurous freedom. And I would not see Maman. Not soon.

Or, as it turned out, not ever.

From that point forward I was, in fact, a fugitive, like Dante wandering through hell, though unlike Dante, I was not seeking a paradise. I did not believe there was a paradise. I had always roamed, barely attached. And I had always survived. That is a thing to remember. I always survived. "It is a kindness that the mind can go wherever it wants," the expelled Roman poet Ovid wrote. Remember that too. Remember that I was in the company of Ovid and Dante, even Byron and Lawrence. Wanderers, all.

~ 5 ~

Paris always seemed to me a city of pale grays—weathered walls and very old streets, while New York is black and white, a place of stark contrasts. I have moved easily in both. But that island jutting into the angry ocean was all shades of white, wind and sea foam, sand and desolation. I lost track. It was morning or it was not. Night lasted days. Days passed in an hour.

Now and then a woman brought food and supplies. She wore a head scarf and thick glasses and said each time, "Here you be then. See you soon." She avoided making eye contact such that I thought maybe she'd been instructed not to. She would glance down at my knees or my feet or maybe at the worn wood of the cottage doorframe. Then she would scuttle back to a beat-up car she left still running out front.

At one point early on, she brought me a suitcase from Bobby packed with the few possessions I had left at the guest apartment—my old coat, for one, and the boots I'd bought from Odysseus. My scarves were not there. I had left my scarves behind on Fifth Avenue. I had left so much behind on Fifth Avenue.

I began to unravel, to recognize the impact of what had happened—the hatred and blood and betrayals. I was so alone out there on the edge of nowhere. I had never in my life been out of a city. I loved even the exhaust fumes and noise of cities, the strangers, high waves of them pounding the curbs and back, their tides moved perpetually by their own wanting moons.

But out there on Montauk the winter moon rose in an empty sky over an empty beach, and in all this unbearable stillness, my dreams began to come dark and terrible. Nobody visited. My identity could not be compromised, and though I knew there was a plan, that Bobby would rescue me in some way, I could not see the plan. And so the specters emerged. They came in the day and they came at night, misshapen faces in queer colors, mocking my miserable life, scolding and laughing in small crowds like a horrific chorus in my head. I could only retreat, take to the bed, and will them away, these monsters of the mind.

They came out of nowhere in that lonely cottage and they have followed me forever. They hide and peek out, ravage and leave, return and return. Even now, these decades hence, they will come some nights, they will creep out of their creviced caves and find me. And when they do, I say I am dying, I say that to myself and anyone with me at the time—and I am not wrong.

But I am not right either, for they do not take me away. I cannot control them, but I can wait them out. Like the winds that beat against the cottage that late winter on Montauk, they come and they go. And I survive, as I said before, though it is a dark survival.

Are you thinking Charles comes back to haunt me? No. These grotesque faces are not Charles, not about ridiculous Charles with his fists in my face. They are a different kind of curse. Like being born on the thirteenth day. Being severed from my home. And being ever obscure. The specters find me because the rest of the world does not. What if I had been saved? What if the audiences had finally known me and loved me, as I suspected they would? What if I had gone from the stage door to my Fifth Avenue apartment abuzz with the afterglow of Nora or Blanche or Katharina? I have rolled about in such possibilities more frequently than I care to admit. Who would not? "The mind can go wherever it wants." As mine did. And still does.

~ 6 ~

My exile on Montauk did not last forever. A car came finally, a young man asked me to get ready quickly, and off we went to an airport somewhere near and then onto a small plane that followed the coastlines of Massachusetts, New Hampshire, and

Maine and across the water to Nova Scotia. We bumped along on every current of conflicting air, propellers, and engines groaning as we went. We did not soar as the plane had from Paris to New York those years before, though for an hour or more I felt free, I did.

We landed in a town called Yarmouth and there the young man who had escorted me, in total silence I might add, waved me off to another man who was neither young nor silent. "Ye come in the still of the night, do ye? Some doings, the old lady say. Bring 'er back, she say, and so I will, tho let me tell ye, missy, thar ain't much to be seen in Yarmouth if ye don't love the sea. And a bit of mud now in the spring, eh? They say Leif Erikson come this way too. Ye hear of that, did ye? Left some stone, tho the missus says Jesus hisself could leave a stone for all that, anything's a story, she say, a stone's a stone, she say, eh?" And on he went, his head bobbing as he talked, his knuckles raw as he gripped the wheel of the old black car he drove.

Yarmouth was merely a stop on my way to Montreal, as it turned out. I had no say in all this travel. On my own, I would have flown straight to a destination and stayed there until the world forgot Charles Bernard and the wife who stabbed him. But Bobby had his own ideas and so he landed me temporarily in the care of his mother's cousin or second aunt twice removed or some such who had imbedded herself into the Lane mythology along the way.

Aunt Cookie lived in a stone house just feet from the crashing sea. Her driver parked me in the wooden vestibule looking up at a grand stairway which Aunt Cookie descended with the grace of a dancer. She was at least eighty and wore a skirt so long it swept the stairs as she came down. I thought her a character from a nineteenth-century play, her gray hair in a pompadour, her collar high and lacy, her fingers adorned in rings. With a small gesture, she had me follow her into a sitting room where she situated herself in the center of a sofa and pointed for me to sit nearby.

If Charles had a penchant for gild and drama, old Aunt Cookie could outdo him on both counts. Her furnishings had been in that room for a century, barely moved I suspected, heavy and dark. Charles at least understood the importance of light. I'll give him that.

"You murdered your husband," she said, fussing a bit with the fringe on her shawl and the rings on her fingers.

"I wouldn't put it that way," I answered.

"Oh? And what way would you put it? Whatever your name is. Of course, they won't tell me that. They didn't tell me you were a criminal either, but I know. I have sources." She lifted one eyebrow. "If you didn't kill him, who did?"

"Circumstance," I answered. "It's what happened."

"Well, there's a philosophy for you. And what will happen now?"

Aunt Cookie asked the right question. Indeed, what would happen next? "I'm sure I won't be here long. Bobby has made plans," I said, thinking at the time that even one day in her mausoleum may be more than my fragile state could bear.

"Let me tell you something, girl. If you're spending time with an old duck like me in a place like Yarmouth, I'd say your days of plans are over. You're in the wind, I'd say. And that's where you'll stay." Her head jutted toward me to make the point, beak thrust for combat.

I gave no reply. At the time, I dismissed her. But, I'll say now, she wasn't altogether wrong.

~ 7 ~

Within days I was flown off to Montreal and scuttled to a shadowy apartment in a very French neighborhood, where I might have been content if circumstances had not left me in such worried isolation. In that close apartment, I had tall windows that opened to a narrow balcony over the street. My view did not compare to the one I'd left behind overlooking Central Park, but still it offered a glimpse outward. I'd sit there for hours, sunglasses covering most of my face, much like Mrs. Goldbloom's veil had disguised me in my disappearance. Remember the play I started to write about the exiled queen? Well, there I was.

One drizzly morning, I saw a man passing below who walked with a familiar grace, tall and elegant, shoes polished I could see, coat fitting his frame to perfection. For a fast moment, I was sure he was Gigi, that he'd managed to follow my tracks and come to change my destiny again, talk me into turning myself in or running away with him to one of his faraway lakes.

I gripped the balcony railing and leaned forward. Would he glance my way? Would he know me in my bleached, cropped hair? I watched him walk freely, a man who could travel any-where in the world without the fear of being followed. A man who could have allowed me to walk freely too, who could have saved me and chose not to do so.

In an equally fast moment, the graceful man turned at the corner and I could see that he was not Gigi. The man across the street had hair slicked back from his face the way Charles had done and features nowhere near as well-aligned as Gigi's. Even so, I kept my eyes on that man walking away until he disappeared, moved into the neighborhood flow and off to whatever life was his own. My breathing eased. But I lost the excitement I'd just had when I thought perhaps Gigi had come to find me, when I thought that some fragment of my old life might still be mine.

Inside the apartment, I rummaged for something I could write on and ended up tearing off a corner of the box my clean laundry had arrived in. On this scrap, I quickly wrote "Do not find me." I wanted to end with an exclamation mark, but refrained from this added bit of drama. Nor did I sign it. Gigi would know. He'd know that I blamed him for my exile and would not let go. I would never forgive him.

When one of my clandestine messengers came by next, I gave her explicit directions to put my note in an envelope, get it to Bobby in New York, and have it delivered to the jewelry repairman named Gigi at the store on Eighty-First and Madi-son. It should not be put in the mail. It should not be handed to anyone but Gigi himself. And when this task was com-pleted, I wanted it confirmed.

It took more than a month before I found a note in a ship-ment of books Bobby sent me. The confirmation said simply,

"Done." I would have preferred the note to say "Delivered" or "Received." Done is so final. What if, in fact, I wasn't done?

~ 8 ~

I spent the next year in Montreal and might have stayed longer if events had not continued to unfold against me. Bobby visited me several times that year, bringing me money and news. I could always hardly wait to see his face, his blond mop and busy energy, his eyes that so clearly adored me. He did not bring me news of Gigi Paulo. But he always had something. Bobby was the type to always know something.

"Your apartment is on the market," he informed me in the autumn of 1962.

"For sale?"

He'd just poured us each a glass of old port, ready to settle into one of our chummy chats alone there in the world. He nodded. "I hear a prince of some sort is interested."

"Why not?" I thought of my husband strutting about his gilded rooms. "Charles assumed he was some sort of royalty after all." Then it occurred to me. "Are all of our things still there? All that furniture—and our clothes?"

"My sources say Claire hired an estate company. They sold the furniture and most of the art apparently. She put away your personal things in storage."

"She did?" I had not thought I'd see anything of my old life again. "I want my scarves, Bobby. The lemon one Claire gave me. And the others I used to wear."

"You want me to take such a risk for a couple of scarves, Corrine? I can certainly replace your scarves for you."

"Have Lafayette Willson's crew contact Claire. They didn't do much else to help."

Bobby shrugged. He never liked it when I lashed out at his mother's lawyer. The best money could buy, Park Avenue, Yale Law, and all of that. But I blamed them for their lack of imagination in getting me free, their complete inability to go beyond the stock moves of defense—and for refusing to let me state my case in the witness box.

"Never mind," Bobby responded. "I'll get them for you."

And two weeks later I received a box in the mail with several of my scarves and two dresses Maman had made for me. Claire had enclosed a letter, written in dark blue ink on pale blue stationery, a reminder that certain charms in her life continued despite her brother's death and my disappearance. I was sure she had written it seated at her delicate desk in the corner of her ordered library surrounded by hardcover books she almost never read. *Dear One*, she wrote, *wherever you are, I hope you are beginning again and thinking of me occasionally. Your mother writes often telling me always of her love for you.* Claire did not sign the note, but penned a small flower at the bottom, a sign of some kind. We were all about signs and secrecy then, all of us.

Wrapped in my scarves and heartened by an old sense of myself, I began to venture out more. At first I'd slink like an alley cat, find a place for coffee or a loaf of French bread, then scurry back to my apartment, legs moving quickly, tail held low. But soon my brash and curious soul grew more confident and I walked farther and longer, finding the types of places I have always prized, the kind where Maman's friends might gather. I dove in and out of such cafés as if I were still a scrappy child on the streets of Paris, watchful but tough, amused and alert.

Many days I forgot Charles or remembered him only as the brother Claire and Maman had teased and shunned. I'd go whole stretches without the picture of his blood gushing onto the black and white kitchen floor and the feel of his body tissues resisting my knife. Sometimes I'd try to recall what his reactions were while I was stabbing him. I had been so absorbed and in such a cloud of rage that, looking back that next year—and all the years since—I cannot see his face. Was he finally frightened of me? Did he realize at that moment that he'd lost? Did he know he was dying? Or did he continue to sneer that I'd even consider him a mortal being?

Not remembering Charles freed me that winter in Montreal, which was a mistake. It was too soon for me to be cavalier. Maybe I was, just then, what Charles would have called "careless." Because people were looking for me.

I knew that the New York City Police Department was keeping a watch on Claire and on those few other individuals who had testified on my behalf. Bobby wasn't sure they knew about him, but he always acted as if they did, though as I've said before, old money does much in this world to aid or abet or protect. Personally, I did not think the New York Police Department was lying in wait for me in the bistros of Montreal.

But friends of Charles were. My arrogant and dangerous husband had pals equal to him. I soon discovered in the thick turn of events that Charles had scooped up money from many of these arrogant and treacherous men in the guise of an elaborate off-shore investment deal. The nature of this deal left no paper trail, of course, so that when Charles died his untimely death, all his so-called partners were left not knowing the status or even the whereabouts of their money. They assumed that I did.

I did not have a regular daily route that I walked, but I had a few regular places. One stormy day I blew into my favorite pub, *ma distillerie* I liked to call it, and as I was stomping the snow off my boots, I caught a quick exchange between the regular bartender and a man at the farthest table in the back. The bartender's eyes went from me to the other man and back to the glass he was pouring in a movement that occurred so fast, I might have missed it. But I didn't miss it. I wheeled around and left immediately, dodged into the doorway next to the pub, and waited to see what would happen.

The man darted out after me, turned slowly in the street to get his bearings, then strolled to a doorway across the street, where he too waited to see what would happen.

The late sun went down. People passed in greater numbers, hustling home from work as the snow continued to fall. I felt my toes go numb, but the man didn't leave and so I stayed where I was in the doorway of that building. I stayed and he stayed and then, suddenly, he was gone. This was almost as disconcerting as his presence.

When a tangle of teenage girls came giggling past me, I jumped out to walk with them. The girls were about my height and moved quickly with much commotion, not seeming to notice that I had attached myself to them. I followed along like that for a long block, then pulled away into another pub, where I downed a whiskey before making my way back to my apartment. I didn't see anyone peering at me along the street, but who knew. The reality was that I had been spotted. Someone had found me.

~ 9 ~

The next day I stayed inside. Snow covered the streets and beyond my windows the city breathed softly, though I did not trust it. From a chair situated back from my balcony, I kept watch all through the morning, mulling over my predicament stuck there in heavenly Montreal with no protection and no allies. Then, sure enough, near noon the man from the bar reappeared, lighting a cigarette outside of the florist shop across the street, shifting his weight, hunched into his overcoat.

I had a phone number that linked me to Bobby through his antiquated Aunt Cookie, of all things. I have no idea if his cloak and dagger methods were necessary, but he meant well and so I went along with him. Seeing the man outside triggered me to use the number and let the anonymous person at the other end know that I had been discovered, that an unknown man was watching outside my apartment, and I would need a way out. "Yes, yes, yes" my contact said to me and when I stopped talking, she hung up.

Spontaneously I went into action. I put on my coat and scarves and walked downstairs and outside, then entered the florist shop directly across the street. I met the man's eyes as I passed him, certain that his face would tell me something and that my physical presence would force his hand. He was not a young man; his eyes had been hardened by something in life or by life itself, which I now see in my own mirror many days when the lighting does not favor. But he didn't speak to me or try to stop me from walking past him. He didn't make a statement of any kind, but seemed to hesitate, as if unsure what to do next.

Inside the shop the scents overwhelmed me for a minute, set me in another season, the roses in bright colors, the flowering plants ahead of spring. I bought ten pink roses that Maman would have loved. The sales girl wrapped them in layers of brown paper, jabbering as she did about the weather in an accent strangely between English and French, while I kept my eyes on the man out front. But as I dug in my pocket for the dollars to pay for my purchase, the man outside drifted away, just as he had the day before.

I returned to my apartment with the summery flowers, put them in a jar I found in the cupboard, and paced. Trouble to me is like weather to an old farmer. I sense it. I feel it nearing or surrounding me. My pulse accelerates. I can hear the air circulate and sounds from far away. I can act without reason in less than a second, change direction, steal the bag of bonbons, flee the courtroom. That is how I knew that someone had come into the building and climbed the stairs to my apartment.

I stopped moving and waited.

"Corrine Bernard? I know you are there." The voice was even and confident, also familiar. The European accent. The commanding disdain. "Charles has money that belongs to other people, pretty wife. Very angry and dangerous people. Do you understand what I am saying? They will not let you wander the globe with their money." He stopped.

"Just tell me how I can access the money that belongs to me and my colleagues, pretty little wife, and I will tell no one that Charles Bernard's murderer is here in a humble upstairs flat in Old Montreal." He laughed like the devil. But he didn't leave.

Charles's friend Ivan didn't leave for quite some time. I breathed without breathing and he stood outside the door with measured taunts and threats. "Do not underestimate me, girl," he hissed through the door finally. Then I heard him descend the stairs. From my windows, I watched Ivan cross the street and enter a car parked at the curb, its engine running and parking lights illuminated. The god's chariot in the darkness and snow. Charles had been a bully. Ivan was more. He was a tyrant who always got his way or destroyed any obstruction. And just then, that obstruction was me.

Immediately, despite the hour, I called my contact again and said that help must be expedited, that I needed to leave before morning. I threw my few possessions into one large bag, wrapped myself in layers, and sat still to be rescued. One

of my messengers came shortly, she too wrapped beyond recognition, her anxious eyes gazing out above her winter clothing. The two of us went out a back exit that I hadn't known
existed and into another car for another journey. In the early
morning, I was put onto the first flight to Saint John's, Newfoundland, where the plane landed in more snow and the
Newfies in the back burst into robust song as we began to
descend.

From above I had my first glimpse of the place where I was
to live for a very long time, its craggy coastline meeting the
wild Atlantic, brightly colored houses climbing small hills,
and snow, as I mentioned, thick snow covering all.

~ 10 ~

Stretches of my life remain in the sharpest focus, even to the
profile of evening shadows, the swirl of my cigarette smoke
in a room, words shouted or murmured or hissed through
the door. Other intervals are wide sweeps, when I awoke day
after day to eat my bread dipped in coffee, did what I did for
so many hours, and closed my eyes at last when the day was
done. Somewhere in that blur of time a country may have
rioted, a despot risen or collapsed, a discovery made to cure
some disease, the earth shifted an iota beneath us.

I arrived in Saint Johns that snowy dawn in 1963, running
from Ivan and his dangerous chums. I left in 1996. All those
years I lived on the second floor of a bright blue wooden
house on a hill in the center of town. The man on the first
floor, a musician and erstwhile military man, had been hired
by Bobby to be on guard. He'd survived significant injuries in

the second world war, burns on his face and neck, and so he chose to stay away from most people. He did not ever need to muster his military prowess on my behalf, but I'd been assured that if required, he could have snapped the likes of Ivan in two pieces and set them neatly outside the door.

He played the cello for hours every day and so, for that long time of my estrangement, I listened to the age-old sad tones of his music for some period in the morning and again at night. I remember most listening to his playing on those occasions when I lay in bed paralyzed by my nightmares, the faces that mocked me and the darkness that came with them. Then, in the haze of those terrible visions, I'd hear my neighbor's melancholy tones rising from below and filling my rooms. And I'd be certain we were dying together.

The people who lived around us seemed to tolerate our separateness, the way we both, for our differing reasons, avoided their congenital affability and went our ways, him playing his mournful instrument and me marching through town to the outskirts like a pilgrim on crusade. And march I did. I marched in the rocky countryside of Saint John's for more than thirty years, knowing that if I so much as met a stranger's eyes, I'd be pulled into a friendship for life, for that was the nature of the townsfolk.

I was a dearie at the bakery, a darlin' at the meat market, a wee thing at the coffee shop, and so on. The good folks of Newfoundland never met a stranger they didn't want to pull into their circle and convert to one of their own. "How do you expect me to remain anonymous in a place like this?" I complained to Bobby that first month.

"Hide in plain sight," he answered. "Face it, Corrine, it's the most unlikely place for you to be."

I remember not agreeing. I hated the smallness and the utter, utter remoteness. But in time I came to love being surrounded by the wild ocean, the jagged prehistoric rocks that formed much of the island, the clear sky at night, and the boisterous, bold colors of Saint John's.

Bobby's visits punctuated those years. He'd fly in on the last flight from Toronto each time, arrive at the back entrance of the house, and bring me scads of treasures, anything from money to kiffles he bought at the Hungarian bakery on Madison. Of course, he could not bring me freedom or Maman or my name in lights on Broadway. But he did what he could for me and one year followed another. I walked miles almost every day no matter the weather. I imagined myself a Thoreau of sorts, thinking deeply and moving along without disturbing the universe. "Love the land but own it not," as he said. That was me then. Perhaps it was the only time I wasn't disturbing the universe.

At least I wasn't locked in a prison, I'd remind myself. I hadn't been tortured to death for information by Ivan and his posse. I will tell you honestly that I did not push to escape Newfoundland the way I'd pushed against poverty in Paris and insignificance in New York.

In September of 1966, in a late afternoon when the freshest breeze blew through my windows and the cellist had begun again to play his Bach sonata, Bobby and I sat face to face in chairs near my front windows. "Lafayette Willson called me this week," he said.

I raised my eyebrows. "And?"

"He wanted me to know that the statute of limitations on second-degree murder in New York is five years. Which is almost now."

"And?" I repeated.

"You could go back."

My fingertips tingled. "What about first-degree murder?"

"You didn't plan to kill Charles. Good god, Corrine. If you'd planned it, you would have come up with a better scheme than stabbing him in broad daylight minutes before the cook showed up." He shook his head in disbelief. "Of course it was not premeditated. Good god," he said again. "You could go back."

I looked out the window to track a cloud moving across the sky. The cello notes grew large and tapered, the bow rasping against the strings in a way I'd come to know meant that my neighbor would begin again, try again, work until he got it right. From the corner of my eye I saw Bobby's crossed leg bouncing around with impatience.

"Corrine. You're not some cold-blooded killer. You were abused. You retaliated."

Bobby could only see me through his good-natured lens. He couldn't understand my relationship with Charles any more than Gigi Paulo could. Or Claire. Only two people in the world ever understood that relationship.

"What about Ivan and the boys? What will be the statute of limitations on them do you think?" He had no answer. Even Bobby, with all his contacts and reserves, could not shield me from the likes of Ivan if I returned to New York. We had both taken many precautions those years to watch for retaliation from Ivan. "I'm better off here," I said.

So I remained.

RETURN

~ 1 ~

I was no longer young. It happened over years, but I saw it suddenly on a day I'd been rambling along the rocks outside of town. The winds had blown a bit of dust into my eye, and as I stood at my bathroom mirror trying to remove whatever it was, I noticed a new face. I leaned in close to my reflection and the light shone directly on me, revealing small changes, lines and sun spots, a weathered rather than dewy tone. I was as startled as if I'd encountered Charles out in the street. Like I'd seen a ghost—only the ghost was me.

That was the fall of 1995, and though I had turned fifty-five on my ominous June 13th birthday, I paid little attention. The years unfolded meditatively for me in Newfoundland. Claire's money or Charles's money and surely Bobby's sustained me and allowed me to eat and drink as lavishly as I chose. I collected books and small pieces of local art that lined my walls and shelves like a squirrel's winter stores. I had everything I needed and my nightmares came infrequently. I drank my last glass of whiskey each evening listening to my neighbor's deep and somber cello.

Want is another matter, for I continued to always want my freedom and after that I wanted fame and deep within, I never stopped wanting to see Maman again. Living those decades in exile I dared not think long about my wants. I did not think about time either. I forgot to count, disregarded the years because all stood still for me. I lived on an island far from anywhere and walked my various paths and wore my same old coat and let my hair blow free in all weather. I had the occasional lover, saw Bobby more and more often as the years progressed, but there was no crescendo there. No arc of promise and culmination. I didn't expect the world around me to be bounding along when I so clearly was not.

In exile, I decided, time had stopped. My heart kept beating and the tide continued to blast the rocks daily and I accepted this. Then I saw my aged face in the mirror.

And then Ivan Vladimir Kuznetsov was arrested in New York City.

Bobby happened to be in Newfoundland when it happened, attached to his sleek computer, and he thumped up my stairs at midday panting with enthusiasm. "That Ivan who threatened you, that Russian crook? They got him."

I looked up from my book. "Who got him?"

"The Feds I think. Or maybe the city, but it's unbelievable. They got him on counterfeiting, embezzlement, and money laundering. Jesus. Probably bodies in the East River too. He'll never see the light of day." He flopped into his favorite of my chairs and sighed deeply. "So now you can go back." He grinned with excitement. "You can audition for plays, live in my penthouse, eat out with me in real restaurants. Wow. Thank god." He closed his eyes in satisfaction. "Jesus."

Ivan in prison. I loved the very thought of it. Pretty wife that I was, I had outlasted him too. "I wonder if he ever found that money Charles invested for him," I mused.

Bobby slapped his leg. "I'm just imagining going to the theater with you. *Hamlet* is on Broadway, Corrine. There's so much—the world's our oyster now."

"Is it?"

He laughed at my reticence. "Yes, it is."

~ 2 ~

But I did not fly away immediately. I had become estranged from the world beyond, knowing instinctively that I would not be *actuel* anymore. I was not young. Acting classes would be full of ingenues with dreams as large as mine had been, and the coffeehouses in the Village would have been transformed to who knew what, vintage clothing shops or expensive restaurants. A prince from somewhere might still occupy my Fifth Avenue apartment, if he hadn't already sold it to a movie star or another mogul like Charles. A man named Bill Clinton had become president of the country, eating hamburgers in the White House and playing a saxophone on television.

It was a different world, and so I held back.

"It's better than before," Bobby coaxed. "You're free. And you have me." He didn't understand my hesitation. "Joanne

Woodward is still alive. Broadway's still there and Rockefeller Plaza. The merry-go-round. You're not thinking clearly."

"I could still be arrested."

"No, no. It's too far in the past. Mother has a new lawyer who assures me. He's brilliant, Corrine. I promise you."

There is something to being a wayfarer, to calling no one place unequivocally home. We do not look back, we travelers in all evenings. We watch the road ahead and, finally, that is why I decided to leave Saint John's. Not to return to a life I had followed thirty years before, but to move on to whatever was next.

"I want to visit Maman," I announced on Bobby's next visit. "I want to go to Paris and then someplace else, maybe London. I have a school friend I might find in London." Bobby gave a headshake of disbelief. He had never known me to have a friend other than him, and I had never told him about Marguerite. I was not sure he would understand her eccentric wildness, her lady lovers, or our oddly intimate relationship. Or maybe I just liked keeping the thought of her to myself. "We used to read books together," I said and left it at that.

I had started writing to Maman years before, when I was convinced that being the mother of a fugitive from justice would not harm her. We no longer exchanged postcards, but sent letters sealed in private envelopes that passed through Bobby and his mother's assistant. She had been thirty-eight years old when I last saw her, younger than I was when our correspondence recommenced, but I could tell she was the same, her words in flowery, predictable script told me of her sewing projects, a few lustrous gowns and many straight hems, her friends still stopping by for their cheery exchanges, and Hubert retired but busy playing belote and rummy with his chums.

Through her letters I learned that the Roche cousins had sold the boulangerie to a young couple who had struggled and, after a few years, had themselves sold it to a Danish baker. She was still grappling with that fact, even though he apparently made perfect breads. "But he is not French, Mimi," she wrote, and I could hear her dismay off the page just as I could hear the lilt in the rest of her words, that musical exuberance that was always hers.

So we made plans. Bobby insisted I pack my belongings and have them shipped back to New York where he would hold them in storage for me until I settled somewhere. I knew that the only place he assumed we would settle was New York, which was home to him, where his mother still lived nearby and his mother's sister and their attorney, of course, and their accountants and advisors and doctors and so on. But I did not have those ties. I had been on a remote island for more than half my life and in three other major cities for the other half. Even so, I did as he asked. My belongings meant little to me anyway.

We left together from Saint John's in the early spring of 1996, just as the snow was breaking up and beginning to melt. In Paris, I knew we'd find flowers and boxwoods and color that I hadn't seen in months. Bobby had arranged a hotel, some grand old place, where we would stay for as long as I wanted, he said. He had visions of us easing into our visit, shopping a bit for lovely things, buying Maman gifts, and resting up from our trip. But that wasn't my vision.

When we were still in the air above the French countryside, my breathing began to race and my feet flexed impatiently in my boots. I was back. It was true and within an hour, I would rush up those two flights to my maman in her cluttered, cheery rooms and look into her merry face and be who I might have been. With every inch that the plane dropped, every cloud we descended through, I got closer and breathed faster. They are some of the clearest hours of my life—that plane landing, the unnerving lines at Charles de Gaulle, the reckless taxicab ride into the heart of Paris.

"Now turn here," I commanded, back in my native territory and remembering my way after nearly forty years. "Now left, here, here." We pulled up in front of the boulangerie that looked so much the same from the curb that I was sure I'd find the Roche cousins somewhere within. I leaped up those stairs and when I reached Maman's door, I turned the knob to let myself in, imagining that I'd catch her off guard at her sewing machine, perhaps, or chopping carrots for one of her soups. Instead, I found the door locked.

I'd written, of course, as we'd made our plans over months, so how could she not know I'd be there that day? Still on fast forward, I knocked like crazy, calling, "Maman, it's me. It's Mimi. Maman?"

You recall how I'd known that Ivan Kuznetsov was in my hallway in Montreal? Standing outside my old door in Paris, dust swirling lightly in the sliver of late afternoon sun coming in at the landing, I knew with that exact instinct that my maman was not there and never would be. Something had gone terribly wrong.

I hurried downstairs into the bakery. "Madame Ramus—where has she gone, please?"

The wiry blond behind the counter covered his mouth with both hands. "*Elle est morte,*" he said, barely a whisper. "*Désolé, désolé.*"

I leaned across the counter to grab his arm. "What happened. She was my maman, she knew I was coming. We wrote, she knew." I am not usually excitable, but at that moment in the boulangerie, I roared like Lear on the moor, I swear I did, the anguish more than anything I had ever known.

The skinny gentle baker held my hands across the old wooden counter. "Something," he answered, his eyes bewildered and distressed. "She got sick. A fever?" He seemed to want me to answer. "Something. She went to bed. She never woke."

At this awful, incomplete story, I bellowed louder, so loud that the Danish baker moved quickly to lock the shop door, then tried his best to comfort me. "*Je suis vraiment désolé,* I am so sorry," he continued to say, murmuring on about Madame Ramus and her joy, her love, her beautiful work. But I couldn't listen, couldn't believe this stranger's news.

"Where is Hubert?" I interrupted.

"He is here."

"He is not here. There is no one upstairs."

"But he is here. He will return. He comes home."

I let myself out of the boulangerie, unlocking the door as I had so many early mornings when I was young and the streets were just awakening and Maman sat at her table in the apartment above drinking her first cup of coffee and milk. I signaled to Bobby in the waiting cab and watched him hop out so blissfully unknowing.

"Maman died, Bobby. She is dead." I looked in panic up and down the winding street, as though some god would arrive to reverse this truth. "We have to wait for her husband to find out what happened. We just wrote, we made plans," I continued to say. I think I said more. I talked in near hysterics, sobbing and hollering, who knows what I said.

We sat in the cab, the meter running into hundreds of francs, I supposed, and just before dark, Hubert came home. I recognized him immediately, for he had the mussed sort of kindness about him that Maman would have loved. From a distance, I could see that his pants were tailored and his sweater knit with cables, Maman's sort of professional details. As he neared I could also see his wispy, thinning hair and pale eyes.

"Hubert?"

~ 3 ~

He recognized me instantly. "Mimi!"

I nodded and he nodded in return, but he did not speak. He signaled for us to follow his heavy steps as he led us back upstairs and into the apartment.

There I experienced the second shocking loss of the day, not equal to the news of Maman, but connected to it. She wasn't there and neither were the rooms I had known so well and had carried with me through every episode and difficult day of my life. The flowered wallpaper had been stripped and the walls painted a bright yellow, my bed under the eaves had been replaced by a tattered chaise lounge covered in the kind of striped fabric you find on old bed pillows and those same stripes also covered a sofa that was not the one I'd sat on with Marguerite as we argued Anna Karenina's choices. Maman's sewing corner had been upgraded and organized, the scattered bins exchanged for a stack of quaint baskets and there was little clutter.

Bobby stood by me as we listened to Hubert tell the story of Maman's headache and the doctor's recommendations that she rest and the way Hubert made her tea and put cool cloths across her forehead and how she slept so deeply and never awoke. I gripped the corner of the large table, the only piece of furniture that remained from my childhood. I did not want to be there. Nothing was right. I'd lost everything I thought would never end, and I didn't know Hubert or find my maman anywhere in him. Despite the clothes she had made for him and the ring he wore that must have matched her own, he was a stranger to me, a brokenhearted stranger whose wife had hung crisp new curtains on their windows and died in her sleep.

He offered us wine or coffee, and when I said I needed to leave, he excused himself to the tiny bedroom and brought out two of Maman's things, which I like to believe she herself had folded and stacked so carefully. One was a sweater that Hubert said she had made to give me on my visit. It mimicked the bright red sweater I had favored as a girl, with cables like

Hubert's sweater and white pearly buttons up the front. The other item was the rose cashmere scarf Claire had given her when she left Paris for New York.

I put both on immediately and shook Hubert's hand. I knew I should have kissed him on the cheek, that Maman would have wanted me to do that. But I did not.

Nor did I stay in Paris. Ignoring Bobby's pleas, I asked the taxicab driver to bring me back to de Gaulle, where we sat all night waiting for an early flight to London. I chose an aisle seat on the plane and studied the rows in front of me. I did not look out the window to watch Paris disappear behind us.

And I have never gone back.

These years later everyone is connected and had this happened now, Hubert could have reached me quickly. But at that time Claire did not even have my phone number. I had been in hiding for so long and had taken on such levels of precaution that news reached me in calculated steps from one place to the next. Hubert had phoned Claire, of course, but she did not know how to contact me quickly. Bobby's mother's assistant, Beatrice, still going strong, always acted as an intermediary and so the news of Maman came to me when it was too late. I had already left for Paris. And Maman had already been buried in the Ramus family plot outside the city.

I had so many chances. I could have gone to see her so many times, used my fake passport, heard her exclaim "Mimi, *mon bébé!*" I had just refused to acknowledge time. Like a wicked and rebuffed lover, in return it had stolen the one person I could not bear to lose.

~ 4 ~

London was not inappropriate for mourning. Bobby set us up in a suite of rooms near Hyde Park and, in a sense, we parted ways for a while. His friends from prep school were now running banks or some such about town and he fell in love with the posh part of London, suiting on Seville Row and fine restaurants. We always knew how to be together and apart, Bobby and I did, similar species in the same wood, hunting and gathering in our own ways. I miss that now, that undemanding collegiality. It is another of the many things I miss. Anyway, while he played man about town, I wore black.

For the next several years I wore black in all seasons. My one exception was the red sweater Maman had made for me, which I began to put on in the evenings and keep on throughout the nights. I cannot say how Maman's death changed me, how knowing she was not in the world left me stranded in a far place such as I had never known, not even living with Charles, not even in exile. I am still ferocious, of course, but I have experienced this massive defeat now and it has marked me. Like the crevices in Lincoln's face, forfeitures even in victory, the ravaged heart of wisdom. Something like that.

And London understood. It provided me the Tower where so many had faced their gruesome ends and Westminster where the high and mighty were buried. I saw a Shakespearean play every week, and who knew grief better? The Greek playwrights, of course, and I saw their work too, and when I was not in the mood for tragic blood flowing through time, I went to the Thames and hung over its old bridges to watch the murky water idling along. I walked miles and miles of streets curving this way and that, nothing like New York's grid or even Paris, which roamed but more intimately. London streets led me to far corners and dead ends and into parks and back to the river again.

That spring passed and so did the summer. Bobby returned to New York for a short time to check in on his life and his mother and whatever else he always had going that I never quite cared to know. As soon as he left, I headed for the London Library on Saint James Square to see if I could track down Marguerite St. Louis. It is a stately library, a place of history and literary tradition, and I got waylaid by the books and the reading tables, the low and individual lamps, the quiet corners. By the time I remembered my purpose, the doors were closing and I was ushered out. But the next day I found London phone books and several addresses for people named St. Louis. I made my list and took it back to our old flat to make my calls.

First, let me say I did not want to do this myself. I wanted Bobby's mother's assistant, Beatrice, sitting there with the list, quickly punching the numbers on the phone and asking if Marguerite St. Louis was available. But Beatrice was off in New York calling hair salons perhaps or organizing political lunches for Mrs. Lane and her powerful set. I had hardly talked to anyone for many decades, and I was out of my element. I got messages at the first two numbers I called, somewhat a relief because I didn't have to talk to anyone, but maddening in that they got me nowhere. I listened to the voices, however, and determined they could not be my Marguerite. They didn't sound like anyone Marguerite would know either—too plain, too English, too sweet.

The third number was something else. "Who is calling?" the scratchy, bossy recipient asked.

"My name is Corrine and I went to school with Marguerite St. Louis in Paris a long time ago. The last I knew she had moved to London. I would like to see her."

"Marguerite left twenty years ago for Australia. She lives in Australia now." I was astounded. Australia is where prisoners went to die, where loose pebbles rolled away to oblivion. "Hello?" came the voice.

"Yes, I see. Well I'm sorry to trouble you."

"She visits occasionally."

"Are you expecting her now?" My heart bounced a bit with that thought.

"No. She was here a year ago. She won't be back so soon. They run a ranch, you know."

I didn't like the idea of 'they' either. "Well, tell her Corrine Milot said hello, if you remember."

"I'll remember," the woman said. "I'm her only cousin. Everyone else has passed on, you know."

Of course, I didn't know. Why do people say such things? If I hadn't talked to Marguerite since 1957, I could hardly know who in her life had died in the interim. "I wish her well," I added to be polite.

"I do too. It isn't easy running a ranch."

"I'm sure it is not." I tried again to end the call. "Thank you for your help. I'm sorry not to see her."

"They have cattle," this infuriating person continued. "Can you imagine?"

I thought of Marguerite, tall and fluid, with her bad eyes and love of the humble pleasures, riding a horse and chasing down her cattle, face brown and hair as wild as it used to be. "You know," I replied, "I actually can imagine." Then I hung up quickly before she could go on.

I filled the bathtub with hot water and oils and slipped into it feeling a passion I had not experienced for many years. Marguerite. I spun my fantasy and gave myself pleasure until the water turned cold and my dreams as well. Marguerite, my friend, my counterpart, my muse. How had I let her go?

~ 5 ~

This pursuit of Marguerite piqued my interest about others who had slipped away. When Bobby returned and we were seated before the fireplace, I asked, "How was New York? Tell me something new."

"Well, Mother's grand. Heading to Paris for the holidays as it turns out. Cousins of cousins." He grinned. Bobby always found his family's web of moneyed relations enormously humorous, an ongoing source of rollicking stories and unlikely characters.

"Is there still a jewelry store on Madison and Eighty-First?" I surprised myself with that question.

Bobby swirled his drink and recrossed his long legs. "The one where we delivered the note for you? No, actually. I believe it is a lingerie shop now. Or folk art. Americana and the like?" He couldn't quite remember.

"Do you ever hear of a singer named Bella Paulo? Wait. It was something else like—Paul? Ever hear of Bella Paul?"

He popped out of his chair. "There's a thing now, sweetheart, called the Internet, where one can search for anything. I've been doing it for years." He grinned again, loving this one up, and pulled his sleek computer out of his bag. I sat in some fascination while he busied himself with plugs and connections. I was curious about Bella Paul, but more interested in her brother. Gigi would have been almost sixty just then, and he surely would not show up on Bobby's computer. He would have left New York for his woods and lakes. Anyway, what would I say to a man who had ruined my life?

"Found her," Bobby said, carrying his computer over to show me her picture. "Retired, it says. But she shows up anyway. Not bad." I took in the photograph of a woman who looked much as I remembered Gigi's sister, though I only saw her once. Time had been good to her, given her a certain aplomb, head held high, glittery dress draped just so. "Too bad I never heard her sing," Bobby went on. "I love this whole World Wide Web business. I'm on here too. I'll show you."

And sure enough, Bobby showed up in his youthful splendor, blond hair half covering his face, an heir in the family dynasty. "What else you want to know?"

I wished that day that I had paid more attention to people's names back when. We could have searched for Billy Jo, the showgirl, or fickle Odysseus or the acting teacher who testified at my trial. For the hell of it, I asked him to look up Marguerite St. Louis, but she was not on Bobby's World Wide Web. And though I was curious to see what might be there about Charles and me, I didn't ask. I poured another whiskey instead.

"Ivan Kuznetsov is waiting for his trial," Bobby said, still typing and clicking and searching.

"So he's out on the streets?"

Bobby rolled his eyes. "Hardly, I think."

Still, he knew what I was asking and was choosing not to answer me honestly. "Maybe we shouldn't stay here," I said. "Maybe London is too obvious."

Computer perched on his lap, he threw both hands into the air. "It's perfect! London's harbored fugitives forever. Hasn't it?"

He didn't know, of course, because Bobby wasn't a student of life. Facts were immaterial to him as were most books, politicians, religions, and philosophies. He preferred to live rather than think about it. Through all the years when I had walked and read and pondered, Bobby romped about doing things I rarely acknowledged, playing squash and tennis, watching the Knicks on television, following music trends, and befriending other rich, intriguing people with time and time to play.

"This city has plenty of darkness for you," he said cheerfully, like this was a good thing. "It's you." He hung on waiting for affirmation.

I recall smiling in concurrence. "I'm fine," I said, "but I'm thinking nobody would ever look for me in a place like Denmark. That's something to consider too."

"Denmark?"

"You have heard of it?"

"Jesus, Corrine, that's like going back to Newfoundland."

"Well, Ivan can't live forever," I said to be conciliatory.

He packed away his computer and adjusted his silk tie. Bobby loved his silk ties, knotted loosely to remind the world that he stood ready to either rock and tumble or meet the queen at a moment's notice. He had never aged, but remained thin and agile, his hair fine and floppy, his face the same except for the tortoise-shell cheaters that perched on his nose when he read the newspaper's sports and entertainment sections. Bobby was breezy and kind and constant. I thought he'd always be there for me.

But on this important point, I proved wrong.

~ 6 ~

That winter I learned how dearly the English love their Christmas holiday, their Christmas puddings and boozy cakes and geese and trimmings. Everywhere I wandered, I was reminded of imminent festivity, this time of color and abundance. Maman would have joined right in, I knew. Knit herself a

Christmas jumper and sang "The Holly and the Ivy" in perfect pitch.

Bobby made plans for us. Certainly I would want to light a candle for my mother at Saint Paul's on Christmas Eve and have tea sometime Christmas week at the Savoy, as who would not? He insisted I come with him to the Covent Garden market for sausage rolls and Stilton, and he paid a young man to string lights across our mantel and hang an evergreen wreath on the door.

"I haven't celebrated Christmas since I left Maman in Paris," I commented on Christmas morning, as I regarded the small stack of presents he had bought for me. "Charles and I did nothing. In Montreal and Newfoundland, I did nothing."

"That's because I wasn't there. It's a grand holiday," he replied. "Give it another try."

He gave me lovely gifts, the kinds of things Claire would have chosen: a black cashmere sweater and matching socks, two bottles of Peated Single Malt Whiskey (England's finest, he relayed) and a limited edition of *Don Juan* by Lord Byron, complete with lithographs. "He was in exile too," Bobby said, beaming as I unwrapped the book.

"I know," I replied. "Because he was a deviant, Bobby." We both laughed with great hilarity, something I have almost never done.

"And you aren't?" he threw out, still laughing. "Well, merry Christmas anyway." He sat back in his chair, the picture of satisfaction. Such easy satisfaction. I've wondered since what sort of soul knows that kind of unquestioning contentment. Not mine certainly.

On Boxing Day, Bobby left London to meet his mother and her distant relatives back in Paris. I had gone for a stroll about Hyde Park and returned in time to see him in his dashing tweed coat disappearing into a taxicab. He waved gaily as the car passed me by and called out the window something about the new year. Back in our flat, I found he had ordered me a pot of tea and warm toast which were waiting on a silver tray. The fire had been lit and the tiny Christmas lights plugged in and twinkling. I settled in to read Lord Byron. And so Boxing Day slid by me.

As did New Year's Eve and New Year's Day, the city abuzz with a revelry that kept me inside and alone. I slept too much and stood often at a window without really seeing what was there. The year of Maman's death rolled into a year she would never know. Marguerite lived in Australia and Bobby had been gone for a week. And then almost two weeks.

Beatrice caught me in midafternoon, when I was well into a pack of cigarettes and an absorbing read of *Bleak House*. "Are you alone, Ms. Bernard?" I hadn't heard her eloquent diction in years, that way she had of overemphasizing consonants.

"I was reading," I answered. "Bobby's not here."

"Yes, I know. Bobby had an accident in Paris." She stopped deliberately.

"He's hurt?" I reached for another cigarette.

"Yes. He was very badly hurt." She stopped again.

"You are telling me that Bobby died?"

"I am."

She did not go on, but waited. She waited for me to crumble, I suppose, and I might have, but the cigarette steadied me. "What do you want me to do?"

"We are taking care of everything," she said and her voice became more forceful, more sure. "The body is in New York now. It took us some days to realize you would be there in London not knowing. We do not want you to jeopardize your safety for this, Ms. Bernard. Stay where you are. Mrs. Lane said to assure you that you will be taken care of, the flat and anything you need. You were her son's dear friend and he would want you to remain safe."

They didn't want me at his funeral. I would never see him again, not even in death, just as I had not seen Maman. Without comment, I quietly hung up the phone.

I opened two large windows to air out the thick smoke that had accumulated over days. I showered and pulled on the sweater and socks Bobby had given me for Christmas and a pair of the drapey wool trousers he'd left behind in his closet. All these years since, I have worn the clothes Bobby did not pack for his trip to Paris. I've never had his navy top-coat cleaned. It would steal his scent away from me—my dear Bobby and his lime colognes.

By nightfall, I was already so much older.

~ 7 ~

The facts of Bobby's death emerged later and were, as the facts in all deaths, dwarfed by the finality itself. He had driven his mother and one of her elderly cousins to lunch with friends in the Sixteenth Arrondissement. The weather was bad, a mix of snow and sleet, and after he parked the car, he stepped into the street, bounding as he always did, I think, and was hit by a truck barreling along unexpectedly through the exclusive residential neighborhood. Beatrice said he died instantly. Without pain or knowledge. Those were the facts.

The truth was something else, as it always is. A moment too soon or too late, a step too quick and too far, the sleet blinding, the swerve inevitable, the lingering ribbon of want that followed. What is a fact? A wife stabbed her husband. What is the truth? If she hadn't won, he would have. Facts are never the truth. They are not even close.

I learned all of this when Beatrice called to report on the funeral service and the financial arrangements the Lane family was making on my behalf. It occurred to me as I listened to her that I had not been poor since I left Paris when I was seventeen. I had so fiercely fought the shadow of poverty, the thin soups of my wartime childhood and lean opportunities thereafter. I had not considered that even in an elegant London flat with food arriving daily on a silver tray and a maid bringing clean towels and a butler of sorts lighting fires in the fireplace, I would not be happy. That my fate would still leave me on the outside, friendless and restless and coiled to strike. But so it was.

For weeks, I left everything of Bobby's in place—his shaving brush and fancy combs, his cardigan tossed over the chair to the desk, his magazines and seldom-used Mont Blanc fountain pen. He had a pocket radio and extra pajamas, fine cotton underwear, a second watch and so on. It wasn't just that I was trying to keep him alive in those rooms we had shared. But they were not my things. Was I to hold onto them all, not just the trousers that somewhat fit me and the overcoat I loved, but all the doodads and expensive supplies? Everything?

Only in early spring did I make a phone call to Beatrice at the number she'd given me to use if I had difficulties. It was a disingenuous offer. She hoped to never deal with me at all. Each month someone in the Lane family circle of support would deposit my allowance in an account and in exchange, well I knew, they expected me to go my way and leave them alone.

I did not reach Beatrice but left a message. The next day a man with a very young voice returned my call. "You can keep anything Robert left behind," he said nervously, his voice breaking to a higher range.

"Even his diamond tie clip?" I asked.

"Oh," he giggled. "Well, that's what they said." He giggled again and hung up.

So for the time I was in London, I kept it all. Even the imaginary diamond clip.

~ 8 ~

At the time of Bobby's death, I was already grieving Maman, already wearing black and looking backward at what had passed in my life. Like me, the city of London stood steeped in blood and history, loves badly destined, dark themes and ancient stories. Dressed in Bobby's trousers, I walked and walked to find my monuments to loss, places where the walls, I thought, would know me and I them.

Though not a great friend of religion, I found myself gravitating to the oldest churches in London, those that had been scorched and abandoned and rebuilt. Churches with names like Saint Bartholomew-the-Great and Saint Etheldreda's, churches with arches and spires and intricate stained-glass windows letting in light in kaleidoscope hues. I sat for hours in the wooden pews of All-Hallows-by-the-Tower, which had taken in many a beheaded body over the years. Though not the most grand, All-Hallows drew me back many times, if only for its willingness to continue. Built in the seventh century and enduring through the Great Fire and two world wars, with only one of its original arches remaining, All-Hallows inspired me. We were of a piece, that old church and I. We were both survivors.

Then by chance I discovered the Foundling Museum, a rococo building full of art and treasures built on the site of the old Foundling Hospital that once housed the orphans and street urchins of London. I tried not to think too much about the somber portraits and picturesque seascapes along the walls or the ornate ceilings and decor. I thought about the children who had been even more alone in the world than I had been, imagining how they maneuvered for food and favor, competed and scrapped and finally found themselves in a warm place where someone, I assume, fed them as they had never been fed before. The very word "foundling" appealed to me. As though those rough street children and abandoned babies were all tiny birds, their beaks wide and waiting. I understood that too.

I frequented the corner pubs and smaller markets, the odd shops that offered hats or ties or buttons. I didn't look for Maman. I am not such a dreamer as that. But I felt her sometimes in those little places where she would have enjoyed herself immensely. I would go back again and again, giving a familiar nod to clerks and bartenders and the like. I bought old books whenever I saw them and gloves of all kinds for some reason. Maybe I was thinking about the crimes I might commit and leave no fingerprints. Fugitives think like that.

I continued seeing plays, as I had since we first arrived in London, often imagining that I would perform this part or that, putting myself into the characters as great actresses might. The Royal National Theater spun out a repertoire that kept me returning. In 1997, I saw *King Lear* there. In fact, I saw it three times, pulled in by the mad king and his irrational outbursts, his unwillingness to face the truth and, in the end, his demise. I couldn't get it out of my head. Of course, I'd read *King Lear*. But seeing it there before me, watching the madness unfold, I recognized something familiar, though even now, I cannot tell you just what was familiar. Not me. Not Charles. Perhaps some amalgamation of our furies or perhaps the same willingness to risk everything to win. I've saved the playbill through all these years. *King Lear* at the National Theater.

It was another play, however, that altered my course, a modern thing called *Copenhagen*, written by someone I don't even recall. It ran on the National Theater's Cottesloe stage in 1998. The spirits of two physicists—Werner Heisenberg and Niels Bohr—sat on the nearly bare stage to discuss nuclear power and such. Bohr and his wife lived in Denmark and Heisenberg had come to visit. This was at the time when Hitler was on the rampage, Denmark was occupied by the Nazis as my Paris had been, and the Gestapo was keeping an eye on both important scientists. All intriguing, but what stung me and sent me back to that flat of mine in some disarray was the question Bohr's wife asked as the play opened. "Why," this Margrethe Bohr says, "did he (meaning Heisenberg) come to Copenhagen?"

Then the play searches for the answer. Why do we do what we do? At the end of *Copenhagen* there is no resolution to this, and so I sat alone for days wondering why I did what I did. How I always said that Charles and I did what we did. We do what we do. But why? Why, for example, had I stayed in London? Bobby had been gone well over a year. I knew no one and though I loved my old places, and London's mists and pervading melancholy, I could not answer the question as to why I was there any more than Niels Bohr and Margrethe could answer why his German mentor had come to visit them in Copenhagen.

Those awful faces began to flood my sleep again, leaving me exhausted and scrabbling for escape. I needed to move on. I needed fresh air and maybe the sea again. So I called a travel agent and, in the span of one fast week, I was on my way to Denmark.

It made no sense. I'd mentioned Denmark in jest to Bobby, simply because it was a place I knew he'd never want to visit. Another take on Newfoundland, as he had suggested, pretty, perhaps, though remote and cold. The play *Copenhagen* was still on my mind, the physicists and their philosophical questions. That's how I decided. And though I had never made my own arrangements before, I worked efficiently to set this plan in motion. I packed two suitcases and left everything else behind, even Bobby's shaving things and watch. I managed to take many of my old books and the clothes I most needed and a few mementos of London, which after all had been a friend to me. It may have been one of my best friends, all things considered, and we parted on good terms.

~ 9 ~

Denmark was a different story. Something not meant to be, I suppose. I was not prepared for the new level of isolation I felt in a country where I knew no one, did not speak the native language and where everyone I saw looked entirely unfamiliar. It is one thing to be an outsider. It is something else to be a foreigner. And that is what I was.

The travel agency had found me a furnished apartment in Copenhagen, a one-bedroom with a view of the water. I left a clubby old London flat with dark furniture and a fireplace, all wood and texture and comfort. In Copenhagen, I entered white rooms with white shades and pale floors, low sleek furniture in pastel colors and a modernity that I had never, truly never, experienced. "What are you?" I recall asking that barren place. It was a fair question.

The sea or some inlet of the sea was never far from anywhere I walked. A restaurant waitress told me that Denmark claimed 406 islands, and later I thought I should have headed off to one of those farthest away. I should at least have gone outside of Copenhagen, which was possibly too clean for me. But then all of Denmark may have been too clean for me.

Saint John's had the same jaunty colored buildings and almost the same weather, but Newfoundland appealed to me for its wild ruggedness, its realistic understanding that it was on the edge and almost forgotten. I didn't get that feeling in Denmark, where the handsome reserved locals pulled inside of themselves with a tame niceness, a distant politeness, and too much pride in how well everything was going all around them. Charles would have thought them Communists. Claire would have been lost. Maman would have tried to adapt and gone off to make her own baguettes. Truly I could not find a baguette in the city.

I also could not find a bar where I'd be happy drinking alone. Or even a lover out of all those golden men bicycling about with rosy cheeks. Within weeks I understood why the character in the play had asked, "Why did he come to Copenhagen?" Indeed. I had taken it on as a challenging philosophical question when it was probably some version of disbelief. Why would he?

I stayed through four seasons. I am amazed that I did. It speaks to my facility for surviving adversity and maybe to my love of the sea. There is that. But when the new year began and the new millennium with it, I decided to leave.

I had nobody left in Paris, London, or Newfoundland. I had nobody left anywhere except for Claire Bernard, with whom

I had not communicated directly in almost forty years. From my bare white apartment, there in the strange land of Copenhagen, Denmark, I called information and was given Claire's phone number corresponding to her address on Fifth Avenue in New York.

The connection sounded as clear as if we were talking across town. But the woman who answered was not Claire.

"I am calling for Claire Bernard," I said.

The brisk voice told me that Miss Bernard was resting and offered to take a message.

"I am her godchild," I answered. "I will call again in two hours."

I fidgeted aimlessly waiting to call back. I shouldn't have been surprised that Claire was resting. She would be more than eighty years old after all. But the woman who had taken my message sounded too efficient, too much in charge of the situation. I had one person left in the damned cold world and I had to pass through some type of manager to get to her.

When I called again, I got a voice recording to please leave a message.

Instead I called the travel agent I had used in London and had her make my arrangements. Two weeks later, on a day in late February, I flew directly from Copenhagen to New York. I landed in a foggy drizzle which obscured the city from me and kept the skyline in vague shapes that I could not discern no matter how hard I squinted into the mist. As the cabdriver wove in and out of traffic to get me to the hotel, I saw him tossing quick glances my way.

"Visiting someone?" he asked. He was an older man with graying hair, his cap pulled low.

"No. Actually, I used to live here."

"But you left, eh?" He laid on his horn to a passing truck.

"Marital problems," I offered. "Things don't always work out."

The driver met my eyes in his rearview mirror. "You can say that again," he answered.

~ 10 ~

I didn't contact Claire right away, nor did I return to the Upper East Side. I gravitated to the part of the city where I'd always felt most comfortable, the Village where I once listened to folk singing and jazz bands, and along the edges of the civilized neighborhoods that had emerged in the years I'd been gone. Just off the Bowery on Second Street, I found a one-room loft in a rundown building with a couple of sculptors upstairs, a starving actress downstairs, and bruised wooden floors throughout. No furniture. No large view. But lots of history, I was sure. Charles and Bobby would not have wanted to even touch the grimy outside door. It was that primitive.

But light poured through a bank of windows on the south side of the room and the ceilings were as high as those in London and the Fifth Avenue apartment where I'd lived with

Charles. I ordered a mattress and several down comforters from a Scandinavian store in SoHo. All sleek and white, of course. I also bought two ragtag arm chairs at a secondhand store and coaxed the clerk to deliver them for an additional few hundred. "This is more than the chairs," he said with alarm when I handed him the cash.

I could have afforded a much nicer place, purchased a condominium as single people do now. But I was still working on the metaphysics of my reentry. Who was I? Where did I belong? Or, as the Bohrs had queried of Heisenberg, why had I come?

I contacted the Lane family. Beatrice had retired after all those years, but a new assistant sent me the few possessions I'd packed in Newfoundland. I'd forgotten what was there—all those books Bobby had shipped to me over the decades and the colorful paintings I'd bought from local artists in Saint John's, a crude pottery vase, which I filled at once with blue irises from a neighborhood market. It was nearly spring, and I was back in New York. It was not home. But it was my return.

REVERSAL

~ 1 ~

In my decades' long absence, downtown New York had changed, cleaned up its many faces and acquired better clothes. My old neighborhood on Fifth Avenue, however, remained the same, the buildings—massive and permanent—still held their ground, their shrubs well-shaped and flowers in bloom. On my way to see Claire, I paused a long while in front of the building where I had lived with Charles, looking hard for some sign that nearly forty years had passed and the hungry, mean Bernards no longer lived there. But I found no such sign. Not one. Even the yellow cabs hustling down the avenue seemed all the same.

I had not called Claire to warn her of my visit. In fact, after my two failed attempts to talk to her from Copenhagen, I had not tried to reach her again. I had been in New York nearly three weeks and stood then in the foyer of Claire's building, querying the doorman who allowed me to call her apartment. "Miss Bernard's residence," the same brisk voice barked. "May I help you?"

"This is Corrine Bernard. I am downstairs."

"I see." She paused. "Well, come up then," she said and hung up. I took the elevator to Claire's apartment and this woman I'd talked with twice opened the door to me with little enthusiasm. Clearly she ran the household, her clipped gray hair as blunt as her manner. "Miss Bernard is in the library." She assessed me as she spoke. "I'll take you to her."

I followed the stocky woman through Claire's pale yellow living room and into her small and pale gray library, where an old woman sat folded forward in her chair, her lap covered in a blanket and her head tipped slightly sideways so that her eyes could meet my own.

"Claire?" I thought surely it could not be Claire, that some enormous, ungodly error had transpired. "How are you?" I ventured, though it was a ridiculous thing to ask. She was obviously terrible, bent and feeble and unable to move.

"Sit down, Corrine," she said, glancing at the chair facing her own. "Let's talk."

The library was as I remembered, close and comely, books on gray shelves from the ceiling down to the floor, no disorder, no loud colors or lack of elegance anywhere. "I have always preferred this room," I told her, still struggling to remember that this was bright-eyed Auntie Claire who had tread so lightly in her pretty shoes.

"My surroundings have not changed, Corrine. Just me. And you, I assume, as well." She paused to look me over. "You are back."

I said yes, I was back and explained where I was living just off the Bowery, surrounded by artistic types, intellectuals perhaps, the kinds of people I had not known well when I'd lived in New York before. I wrote my address on a notecard, which she instructed me to take out of a drawer in the dainty table between us.

"I will not visit you there," she declared.

"No, of course not. You would not like it anyway." I couldn't take my eyes off her. I think never in my life had I been that close to a person so irreparably afflicted as I saw Claire to be. "What illness do you have?" I asked at last, unable to contain my dismay at finding her so.

She laughed at my question, a loose, almost youthful laugh that reminded me of who she had been. "It's some type of arthritis. And some type of old age. And there's probably Parkinson's in the mix. And the devil as well." She laughed again, but not so lightly.

"I'm sorry."

"Everyone is," she answered. "Most of all me. But you, Corrine, look almost the same. Rather beautiful, I'd say. You have been taken care of?"

I wasn't sure what she meant. "I've certainly not wanted for anything," I said, "other than a free life, that is. So yes, I've been cared for."

"I gave money to your blond friend quite regularly. The one with the expensive shoes. The money belongs to you, really. You were Charles's wife and he died and so it belongs to you. I certainly don't need any more. But I haven't seen your friend in several years. What are you living on now?"

I didn't want to explain Bobby to Claire. I didn't want to discuss the allowance from his family or even what he had been to me. I let her question go. "I'm fine," I said instead.

"You are fine and you are back. Did you make it to Paris before your mother died? My dear Mireille." She uttered Maman's name as a prayer. "Did you see my dear Mireille?"

I told her my awful story of arriving days too late. "Her husband said she had a fever and died in her sleep. I have no idea how such a thing could happen."

We sat and said nothing for a minute. Then out of our silence, she mused, "I consulted two doctors after I talked with Hubert, you know. They seemed to think she may have had something like encephalitis." She shrugged slightly. "There are many kinds of bad luck, don't you think?"

Finally, Claire had acknowledged the existence of bad luck. "I always thought your fate had been cast so favorably," I replied.

She frowned in some type of disagreement. "In what way, Corrine? I am curious to know how you thought I was favored."

"You were never uncomfortable."

"Until now." She grimaced as she adjusted herself slightly in her chair.

"Your father loved and pampered you, you came and went freely, you have lived all these years in this luxury, these pretty rooms, this library, always knowing you could do whatever you pleased. That is a lucky fate, Claire. You must know that."

Still she frowned, her head cocked at that odd angle to look right at me. "You had your mother, Corrine. I did not have a mother. And you got away after all, didn't you? And traveled, I assume. And had your errand boy to dash about on your behalf. That does not seem so unlucky to me."

At that point I wanted Claire, my last living connection, to understand my grievances, my lost and meandering existence. "I have done nothing of consequence, Claire. I have been in hiding more than half my life."

She shook this off. "And now you are here and you are not nearly upside down in a wheelchair, my dear. So tell me where you've been all these years."

"I went first to Long Island and briefly to Nova Scotia, then I hid in Montreal for a year and from there I went to New-foundland for a very long time. I walked. I read books. I waited. After Maman died, I lived in London. I wanted to be in Paris, but I think I am done with Paris. Then I stopped in Denmark for a year, but that was not the place for me."

She nodded slowly as I talked, I presumed imagining this life I described. Just then the other woman appeared in the door-way to declare that Claire needed rest or medications or tea or something. I was, in fact, excused.

"Come again, dear," Claire said to me. "We can converse some more about how our fates have been cast."

"Yes," I agreed, and I thought that I would. But, as it turned out, I did not.

Other things happened.

~ 2 ~

A week or two after the trip to Claire's, I came home from my morning trek about the neighborhood to find a delivery man sitting on the front steps of my building with two sizable cardboard boxes perched on his two-wheeler. "You Corrine Bernard? Got these for you—need a signature." He thrust a clipboard at me, smacking furiously on his gum.

"What are they?"

"From, let's see, Miss Claire Bernard to Mrs. Corrine Bernard." He grinned. "Some relative, hey?" He bumped his cart up the steps, rolled it down the hall and into my lean apartment, where I saw him take a quick glance at the rough walls and worn floor. "Well, take care of yourself, anyway," he said and tipped a hat that wasn't there and left.

The boxes contained most of my wardrobe from the years I was married to Charles, the Cardin dresses I'd sketched for Maman to copy and my skirts and sweaters from Bergdorf's. Someone had wrapped my expensive shoes carefully in tissue along with the strands of pearls Charles had given me. Lavender sachets had been tucked in among the delicately folded dresses and cedar balls placed inside the sweaters.

I was stunned. There, in two boxes, a life I had lived came back to me in minute detail, in bone buttons and silk charmeuse, in the barely scuffed soles of Italian-made shoes. I had not dreamed that life. No. There it was, returned to me, on a new spring morning in New York.

The only mirror I had in the apartment was the one above the bathroom sink, so I was not able to see how my old clothes looked on me. Most of them, except the most-narrow skirts, fit me well. The shoes were all a bit tight, the result of my walking many miles every day in flat, wide boots, but they were still wearable. One by one, I lifted garments out of the boxes, tried them, and laid them out on the bed. Claire had not thought to have whoever filled the boxes also pack hangers, so later that day, I went out in search of appropriately fine wooden hangers, the kind Bobby had preferred.

By sunset I had put my long-ago wardrobe into the closet of that bare apartment near the Bowery. I sat on the edge of the bed, smoked my evening cigarette, and considered the clothes, all with their lightly attached presence of where I had gone and what I had done in those tense, voluble years. The clothes pulled me backward. I wasn't sure that was the right direction for me to go.

~ 3 ~

Then I saw Gigi Paulo.

I had walked out to the front stoop with the actress who lived in the basement level apartment. When I first moved in, I told her that I had once pursued acting in New York, and so she believed me sympathetic to her trials and rejections, her unpaid bills, and worries over audition hats. She was on her

way to a class of some kind and we were having a laugh about
her overly intense acting teacher. "Find your space, Amy, find
your own space," she'd mimicked and waved as she headed
out across the street.

I watched her go—and then I saw him, standing on the other
side of East Second Street, holding a paper cup and looking at
me. I was already trying to adjust to that closet full of clothes
from the past and now here was Gigi Paulo coming my way.

"Hi, Corrine. It's Gigi," he said with a pleasant smile, as
though we'd been neighbors for the near half century gone by,
used to meeting like this on the sidewalk. I couldn't believe
his aplomb.

"Get away from me," I yelled. "Get away!" He didn't move.
"You have no right to show up here when I told you to leave
me alone. Go away!" I shooed him down the street like an
unwanted dog and, because he was Gigi, ever well-mannered,
he turned and began to leave, his step still youthful, his
demeanor so striking. "Gigi," I called after him. "Where are
you staying in New York?"

He looked back at me. "The Stanhope," he answered, and
continued walking away down the block.

I do not believe in signs, in the mysterious powers of the
moon or the weird auras of black cats. But seeing Gigi the
same week that I'd hung all those beautiful clothes in my
closet rocked me out of the heavy solitude I'd carried since
Maman and Bobby died. Gigi and those clothes reminded
me of the illusory side of life, gold charms on Claire's childhood bracelet, the apricot-colored walls Marguerite St. Louis's

mother so loved, Maman's window boxes of long-blooming flowers, bags of chocolate bonbons.

Gigi was such a handsome man.

I picked out a plain black dress from my wardrobe and the least snug black shoes. Then I hunted Soho's fancy vintage stores for the kind of watch that Gigi could admire, finding at last a Baume & Mercier stainless steel chronograph—from the 1960s, the store owner informed me. Of course, the 1960s.

That evening I took a taxi to the Stanhope, a small hotel just blocks away from where I had lived. It was a luxury hotel, not the kind the young Gigi Paulo would have chosen. But time alters all. The desk clerk phoned him, and he came down to the lobby to meet me, not even surprised that I was there. "That's a wonderful watch," he said immediately.

"I paid a fortune," I answered, holding out my wrist for him to examine it more completely. "These vintage watches are not cheap, you know."

"It's a chronograph," he explained as we got into the elevator together. "Works like a stopwatch, if you choose. See the second hand? Makes it very precise. Pilots use them. Astronauts too," he added, reminding me of how he once explained sad music to me and the chemistry of Bolognese sauce, how to water a violet and the attraction of fishing on lakes. Once inside his hotel room, I sat down and, feeling much more comfortable than I had expected, I took off my impossible shoes.

"You look good, Gigi," I said, an understatement to be sure. His blue eyes lit up his face, which was weathered but still smooth. "Not bald or fat," I continued. "Good haircut. Nice shirt." He was more than those things, but I didn't say. I would never say.

"You look good too, Corrine. The years cannot have been too terrible for you on the run."

This was not the best comment for him to make. "I would have preferred to stay in New York, Gigi. I would have preferred you to come to my defense, so I could have stayed and acted and made my mark instead of hiding out in one backwater place after another. Just to be clear."

"You do not look like a woman who has suffered too much," he argued. "You look beautiful."

I considered his compliment. I supposed I was still beautiful, but at what cost. "Beauty comes from suffering," I thought to say. "When you suffer, your eyes expand to hold the tears, Gigi, did you know that? The muscles in your face give in to it, you rise above the pain and, after so many years, you are more beautiful than before." I had no idea where this had come from. A play I'd seen once perhaps or one I'd imagined. I hardly ever cried, truth be known.

But Gigi had stopped listening anyway. His eyes had glazed over and he'd left me, gone to wherever he had been all those years, years he had cast me into exile as he continued to move forward in his life. He could always incense me, this handsome man.

"Are you listening to me, Gigi? I wore these horrid little shoes and came all the way up here to your hotel, and you are glancing out the window. There is nothing out that window, Gigi."

"I'm sorry," he said. "I have a daughter who always wanted me to bring her to New York, but I wouldn't. I never came back until now."

I did not like that he'd veered away from me so soon. Nor could I picture Gigi raising a daughter. I thought of him always as the man who hoped we'd live together forever. "And now you miraculously find the woman of your dreams again in New York City. Aren't you the lucky man?"

He sat on the edge of the bed close to me and I felt such a draw to him, I could not keep my toes from wiggling against the deep plush of the hotel carpet. At that moment one of us, either Gigi or I, could have altered our course. We could have come together freely on the brocade-covered bed and whispered lies and created a different story. But we did not.

Gigi talked about the note I'd written from Montreal my first year of exile, the one telling him not to find me, which was why a million years later he'd decided that he would. Here we are together, he said, all so easy, like this was meant to be.

"You didn't come to apologize?"

He looked as though I'd slammed him with one of Charles's gilded figurines, like he couldn't believe I'd say such a thing. "You killed him, Corrine."

Nobody had said that to me in a very long time. "He was ridiculous," I answered. "Horrible and ridiculous."

Gigi's voice lowered and he leaned closer to me. "You could have married me. I wanted to protect you and take care of you."

"In the Minnesota woods? Are you joking, Gigi? One look at me and you had to know that wouldn't work."

As soon as I said that, I recognized the irony, for where had I spent most of my life but on the edges of untraveled territory, along the rock paths surrounding Saint John's on an island so remote nobody had thought to look for me there for more than thirty years. Could Gigi's woods have been so different? What choice had I made? And as I considered what I chose and what I might have chosen, the grotesque night faces peered in at the sides of my vision.

"I'm dying anyway," I said at last.

He didn't believe me, of course, but the horrific dreams were not untrue and have, both then and now, felt like some version of death come to mock me. "Things lurk, Gigi. You fish on lakes. You should know things lurk."

"Tell me what lurks, Corrine." I did not like his tone.

"I don't think I will, Gigi. Now you've found me and you can remember me in this nice dress at this nice hotel having our little chat about old times. Tell me, what happened to your pretty violet?"

"I gave it to my sister and it died."

I laughed. "Of course. Singers and actresses can't take care of pretty plants. They can barely take care of themselves. How is your sister? Does she know you are here?"

"She lives in Manzanillo, Mexico, now. Nobody knows I'm here. Not even my daughter."

The daughter again. "Tell me about her, your daughter. What is her name?"

"Margaret," he said.

"Ah," I answered, "I knew a Margaret in school. Marguerite we say in French." I told him about my Marguerite and the poem by Gerard Manley Hopkins that is addressed to a child named Margaret. "I'll find that poem for you, Gigi. A poem for your daughter before I die."

He shook his head at that comment, but we went on talking. He told me he'd moved out to live on a lake some years before. He said his wife had died young, that he had worked in a small-town jewelry store for thirty years. I again reminded him that he could have saved me, and we drank a small bottle of wine from the bar in his room. At some point, he asked about Bobby, whom he knew as the blond man out on Madison Avenue, laughing into the wind that winter before the trial. Gigi did have an astute memory. And so the conversation moved back and forth between us.

"I wonder if the bistro by my old apartment is still there," he said and I told him, yes, I'd seen it my first week wandering the city.

"Do you still cook, Gigi? Do you still make your meatballs?" He listed all the foods he cooked for himself there in his house on one of those blue, blue lakes. "Take me to our bistro," I said after his litany of wonderful foods. "Tomorrow night. I'll get a nice Italian wine for us. Barolo," I teased. "Top-notch."

I saw his face get dreamy and hopeful, the face of the young man who painted his table red and played the blues on his phonograph. But I had moved on to the next night, when we would sit in that charming bistro that had always reminded me of Maman. I said good-bye and left on my own, thinking about when I'd had Barolo with Charles or Bobby and where I might go to get a good bottle.

Heading back, I barely noticed how tight my shoes felt on my feet.

~ 4 ~

But I was dying. That night the mocking faces returned with the force of a battalion, overpowering the satisfaction I felt about my trip to the Stanhope, the graceful sweep of the second hand on my old Baume & Mercier and the June moon high over the East River. I shook and shivered and clung to the edge of my duvet as to a life preserver on a torrential sea. Perhaps I had a legitimate fever, some wracking infection or maybe it was something of the devil, as Claire had implied of her gnarled body. Explanations matter little in the throes of war, who crossed what border or opposed which leader or bombed a ship of innocents on their way to visit relations. I have rarely dug for causes. No prognosis will change the outcome. The faces come. Ever since I fled the New York courtroom, the faces have come. Think what you will.

I forgot my date with Gigi, the bistro, and the Barolo, lost track of time altogether. I remained in bed, sleeping very deeply then, off and on, awoke to semiconsciousness. I was vaguely aware of sun in the apartment and then that sun fading and returning. When my mind finally quieted and I came away from the wreckage, I sensed someone in the room.

I sat up suddenly to see Gigi, dressed in a white shirt and dark jacket, standing in the pool of morning light coming in at my windows. "What are you doing here?"

"We had a date at the bistro," he answered, coming slowly to the bed.

I did not want him to see me that way. It was all wrong.

"The door wasn't locked," he continued, "and I was worried."

I had been so expectant and then so ill and now here he was taking away my chance to make an entrance on some other night, to recover the bistro and some bit of magic I had not known in so long. I exploded. "You are always worried, Gigi! Where does it get us?" He could never respond the way I needed him to respond, ever offering me good intentions but not able to save me from Charles or the court or even my fiendish dreams.

"You never face the complexities, do you? Even now, you're almost an old man and what do you see? Your longtime sweetheart. The girl you left behind. All rosy. All dreamy. And if there is a problem, you worry. But here is the thing, Gigi, I didn't plan to have no father or to marry a horrid man. I didn't plan any of it or to roam around without purpose all my life and never make my mark. I'm a ghost, Gigi, a fucking ghost. And you're part of that. All your worries and honesty or whatever you say, you cast me out to wander like one of those lepers in the Bible. Now you come back to see if I'm fine or good or whatever you think I am. I'm not, Gigi. I'm not."

He had frozen in place at the foot of the bed. "Why did you visit me at the hotel?" he asked, surprised and uncertain.

Why had I?

"I have my curiosity," I answered. "I have nice dresses I want to wear." At that, I surprised myself and began to cry, an exhausted and exasperated crying, my weakness after the long night and day and handsome Gigi not able to understand me, not able to go toe-to-toe with me as Charles had done or humor me effortlessly as Bobby had. "Go," I shouted. "Shut the door."

He took some steps away, but stopped and stuck up for himself with a reasonable tirade against me, how he didn't murder Charles, I did, and how he'd kept watch over me all night and what a nice time we could have had at the bistro. He ended by saying, and I have long remembered his exact words, "Maybe I'm a dreamer, Corrine, but you—you know how to ruin everything."

I said nothing in return. He closed the door behind him and was gone.

An hour or two later, I got out of bed. I called the housekeeping service I employed to come and clean my spare space and while the two ladies whirled through their tasks like fairies of old, I pulled *Anna Karenina* off the shelf and began reading it again for the tenth time. I always open the book with great hopes for the consequence. I can never accept the fact that her story ends as it does.

~ 5 ~

I found it odd to be living in the new millennium. It left everything I'd cared for too far behind, as though the old streets of Paris had been ordered into linear patterns and lost their overgrown ivy, and every philosopher and great thinker had blurred before our eyes. I preferred the previous millennium. I still do.

For an entire week after my encounter with Gigi, I stayed inside, ignored the June light and the brave birds in city trees and I read. I finished *Anna Karenina* and despaired. I read *Madame Bovary* again and despaired. All the while I thought I'd hear from Gigi. That he'd send an enormous bouquet of flowers as Bobby would have done or a messenger with a card, as I might have. But one pretty day followed another without word. Finally, I called the Stanhope to see if he was there, if we might still rendezvous for a French dinner.

"Mr. Paulo left this morning," the desk clerk told me with great cheer. He'd stayed in New York a week after I'd ordered him away and never thought to come back to me.

I'd been in New York for several months and what did I have? A sister-in-law collapsed in a wheelchair in her serene rooms on Fifth Avenue and an old lover, as attractive to me as ever, who never said or did what I needed him to do and was now off to his land of lakes.

That night I dressed well and went to the bistro by myself. I bought one of the most expensive bottles of wine on the menu, a Chateau du something or other, and silently toasted everyone I could remember from Stella Cordeau, whose father didn't read, to my cello-playing guardian in Saint John's. I toasted any friend of Maman's I could still conjure and Hubert and however many stray cats he and Maman had nurtured.

I ordered the four-course prix fixe meal and relished every bite, ate as I had not through all my years of mourning. I toasted the men I'd encountered in New York when I was young and our meek cook who had tried to testify in my defense. I even toasted Charles, because he had lost. And Ivan, because he had lost too. I was the victor returned from battle, the traveler back from the sea. In two days, I would be sixty years old and my fires still burned. I could elaborate a new arithmetic, could I not?

I ended my long feast with a toast to myself, to being alone and being alive and, here's the key, being ready. In the stiff new millennium with all its hidden technologies and buzz, I was there in my worn boots with Tolstoy. Dumas. Charlotte Brontë. Kipling. Forster. Flaubert, du Maurier, and Poe. With Byron and Dante, my fellow wanderers. Wordsworth lost in his natural world. Thoreau in his. These companions never raised an eyebrow, never left for blue lakes, or died when I wasn't there to rescue them.

I walked home from the bistro breathing in New York's nighttime hustle and lights and speed. I was going to be a woman of letters. Write my story, dear reader, so that you would know me. Put myself on the library table next to *La Dame aux Camélias.*

That was my plan.

~ 6 ~

Over the next year, I settled further into my space in the East Village, bought bookcases and a desk, an ancient Asian rug raveling at the edges, and I started to write. Almost immediately, I became paralyzed, comparing my pages to all those I'd read so sedulously throughout my life.

I decided I might not be ready. That I might need a stretch of time to read again every book that mattered to me. And so I did, taking hours of each day, buying little reading glasses like Bobby's to perch on my nose, having my early cup of coffee and my glass of whiskey late afternoon. I continued to find books that mattered to me. Why had I never read Joan Didion, for example, with her rhythmic prose and point of view not so unlike my own? And somehow, she led me to Lillian Hellman and Hellman to Dashiell Hammett and Hammett to similar crime writers whose detectives all tried to trick wicked wives like myself. I discovered Toni Morrison and Alice Walker and Maya Angelou too, which took me in a whole different direction. Months and months went by. Words passed through me and on.

I tended to start my days walking, as I had for so much of my life. I walked the lower third of Manhattan, up to Kips Bay and across to Chelsea some mornings, or down to Chinatown, through SoHo and around Greenwich Village other days. Occasionally I walked all the way to the Financial District and watched the very busy types tote their briefcases in and out of the skyscrapers.

These were not the searching walks of my youth or even the ebullient walks of my early years in New York. Since then I had come to know sea cliffs and rocks and many old rivers. I'd been to the edges and stayed there for so long that walking had become a salvation to me. I claimed my own version of the world when I walked, found a shabby bakery on Sullivan Street that sold peppered pretzels and coffee shops tucked into the scenery everywhere. Chinese fish vendors. Italian trattorias.

One morning was not much different than another. On the eleventh of September, I had started early because the light was so particularly bright and the sky so blue. I happened to be near a grade school when I heard a plane unnaturally low, and stopped and turned to watch it. I saw it descend to just above the tallest downtown buildings and then into one of them, as though the pilot had not noticed that a solid structure of steel and glass loomed before him. Within minutes there were smoke and sirens and hubbub around me, a sooty debris high on the air and above that the sky still brilliantly, unsympathetically blue.

When the Nazis controlled Paris, Maman and her friends knew when to get out of the streets. Not sure if all of New York was being bombed that day or if I'd just witnessed a ghastly accident, I ran back to my building. The two sculptors from upstairs, neither of whom spoke much English, met me at the door in panic, and together we went to their apartment and huddled around the small television set they'd propped on concrete blocks in a corner away from their work.

We passed the day in horror, as did all the city and maybe most of the world. Grotesque faces, like those of my nightmares, had been unleashed on all and this was the result, this utter devastation. I did not sleep for nights.

Then before I could think to contact Claire and assure her that I was well, her efficient caretaker called to tell me she had died. Her body had caved in upon her lungs until she could no longer breathe. And so the dark time grew darker.

~ 7 ~

I do not remember what I did those weeks. I did not walk because it wasn't pleasant to be outside. I did not read because I could not concentrate. I moved my books around. I doodled little sketches of things. I sat upstairs watching my neighbors work on their unruly sculpture and I waited. I would not have anticipated how good I had become at waiting.

Sometime then, I heard from Claire's attorney, who wanted me to meet with him about her estate. We set a day in early November and I took a taxi back to the Upper East Side, which had experienced no visible damage in the terrorist attacks. Well-dressed ladies still strolled the Madison Avenue shops. Flags flew gloriously in front of the Metropolitan Museum. Trees stood stark and exposed in the park.

Her attorney had an office on Eightieth Street near Park Avenue, with a wrought iron grate on the door and a discreet

bell. He sat me in a room hung with the very type of paintings Claire always chose—portraits and elusive landscapes, all
heavily framed. Then in a level voice, he went over the details.

In essence, Auntie Claire had left me everything. Everything.
Her eighth-floor apartment with its pale rooms and dark
paintings, her bank accounts and investment portfolio. She'd
portioned some assets to her favorite charities and had gifted
her employee a trust, but the rest she had left to me, her
unfortunate godchild, the sister-in-law who had stabbed her
only brother. Braided fringe we were, Claire and I, entwined
by restless fingers.

The attorney explained many things to me that afternoon. I
signed papers, nodded, drank coffee, nodded some more, but
all the while my mind was slamming about looking for escape.
What would I do with Claire's apartment and all its pristine
furnishings that meant nothing to me? What had she been
thinking to burden me in that way? Claire had bequeathed
me responsibility, that's what she had done. For the first time
in my long life, I owned property and things, accounts and
more accounts.

I left the offices in a daze and walked up as far as East Harlem
and over a few blocks to the park and south again and back
and forth, here and there, paying little attention to any of it.
My mind returned to Claire on the last day she lived in Paris,
her young face anticipating adventure in the new world, her
thrill at the sweater Maman had knit for her and her pleasure
when we wrapped ourselves in the rose and yellow scarves she
gave us. How easy it was to accept a cashmere scarf, toss it
around my neck, and loop it under my chin, feeling the soft
fibers against me. How easy such gifts had been.

"Hey, friend," one of my sculpting neighbors called to me as I came up the stairs to our building. "We are done, you see. You come see." He grinned a brilliant white in his keen dark face. I had become compatriots with him and his cohort, spending odd hours with them, barely speaking but appreciating a similar perspective, I thought. A mutual concern at least. I followed him to their apartment to regard the metal sculpture that rose like a creature in the middle of the space. I had watched them build it, metal and wood, tangled adornments, reaching filaments, watched them arguing over what went where and why, jolly intellectuals, those two. Now there it was. Completed and filling most of their apartment in all directions.

"What are you going to do with it?" I asked. "Where will it go?"

"Museum?" one joked. That is what they hoped, I supposed.

"It's bigger than the doors. You will have to leave it here forever."

"No, no, no. I show you," the smaller, quieter artist began to dive around the sculpture pointing out its seams. "Comes apart here, and here, and moves like this. Moves like that." He beamed at their ingenious pull-apart monster shining mysteriously in the evening light.

"It's beautiful," I said.

The two men smiled. "You want to buy?" They loved to tease. I'd seen them treat their work and themselves as welcome bits of madness vaulting off surfaces, unpredictable and cheery.

They both laughed heartily at their offer. The lady downstairs who didn't even have her own television set.

"Yes," I answered. "I will buy it. How much would you like? Ten thousand? Or twenty-five? I'll give you twenty-five thousand and you donate it to a museum so other people can see what you've done."

"Sure lady," they continued to joke. "Sure."

I had not felt so good in all the five years since I'd lost Maman and Bobby. I was a rich woman. I could fund artists if I chose. Make these kinds of deals readily, buying and selling like Charles used to do. No wonder he'd enjoyed it so much. Already I felt an unfamiliar power, a new arithmetic altogether.

I didn't have full access to Claire's accounts for several months, but when I did, I delivered a check to my upstairs neighbors along with a bottle of champagne. Even then they did not believe it was real. Only after they'd deposited the check in a bank account did they understand that the wandering hermit downstairs had money in her mattress.

~ 8 ~

Eventually I sold almost everything of Claire's, but it took me years and years. I had acquired very little in my life and so had no experience in divestiture. Still I acknowledged that those pale perfect rooms of hers represented a history for me. Maybe the only history I might have. And so I established a routine, whereby I would visit Claire's apartment every Tuesday and

Thursday. I would arrive by ten in the morning with a lunch from one of the various take-out places along the way, and I would stay until late afternoon.

I began in her library. I opened a book, decided if I would keep it, then moved on to another. Every shelf in that library went from the ceiling to the floor and every shelf had its tidy line-up of book after book after book. I didn't choose to keep many of them, though I found a few irresistible. A complete collection of Shakespeare's plays, for example, and photography books like Atget's *The Art of Old Paris* and *Three Seconds from Eternity* by Robert Doisneau. I was intrigued by her many novels in French and English, best sellers that went back decades, and several shelves of art books, artist biographies, antique reference manuals, and the histories of many countries. She had good taste for someone who read so little.

Whatever I didn't keep, I returned to its place, as her attorney had assured me that there was no shortage of professionals who dealt with abundant collections abandoned in the wake of death. "Unlike King Tut," he had commented at the beginning of this arduous process, "we do not take it with us."

After some weeks, this trip to Claire's to methodically dig through her possessions became a way of life. I liked being near Central Park again and the Metropolitan Museum. I liked the old familiarity of the Fifth Avenue neighborhood and the constant hum of traffic rolling by.

But during that period of time, I did not continue reading the many books stacked all over my own apartment, and I did not even think to return to the story of my life. Instead I delved into Claire's, her nineteenth-century art and nineteenth-century copper pots, her matched clothing, and sets of Haviland limoges, as well as the leavings of her later years, those ointments and medications, walking canes and braces. I looked at everything because I didn't want to lose anything that might be important.

It took me a year of such excavating before I found the drawer where Claire had stored all her cards and letters from Maman. Some went back to their schoolgirl friendship, folded notes of endearment, *ma cherie* and the like, silly exchanges such that I could almost hear their giggles. I took my time, reading each word my maman had written, seeing her cursive rise and fall and dally about the pages, intense and worried at times—more times than I would have thought—and resolute at other times. I had my picture of Maman, forged in childhood, when war was behind us and I was her promise and her gray eyes twinkled with charm. I had not considered how she might have changed to accommodate a daughter who married badly and ran from the law and whom she was never able to see again. I'd known I had troubled her, of course. But did I comprehend the continued anguish I read in her letters to Claire? No. Never.

After I read them all, I emptied one of Claire's polished wooden boxes and filled it with Maman's letters. I left it at Claire's until the apartment sold and now keep it on top of the bureau by my bed. I see it every morning when I awake. I see it every night before I turn off the lamp.

Sometime after that, I came across Claire's childhood charm bracelet, the one she'd brought to the jewelry store for Gigi to fix, which he did. That was when he'd followed her to my apartment and tangled with Charles and left me before we

could share a bit of whiskey. It is a pretty little trinket with
five gold charms dangling off a delicate chain. Claire had kept
it in a large leather jewelry case with a tiny lock and key. So
like Claire. The rest of the jewelry did not interest me, but
I took out the bracelet and wrapped it around my wrist over
the watch that I had bought to impress Gigi and have worn
every day since I bought it.

I took the bracelet to a vintage store on Wooster where they
added a few extra links to the chain, then I put it on and let
it clang about as I sorted through the rest of Claire's things.
It was not sentiment that motivated me, unless sentiment is
a story we choose not to forget. For Claire, her bracelet was
a token of childhood, a gift from her dear papa. For me it
holds the story of a jewelry repairman who fastened its gold
charms—a star, the Eiffel tower, and the rest—and went in
search of a girl he thought he could save. It is not a true story
exactly. But it is one I like to believe.

I had promised Gigi Paulo a poem for his Margaret, but that
gesture had been lost in the chaos of terrorism and the sub-
sequent disarray of the neighborhoods near me and then
Claire's death and then all her belongings. But weeks after
finding the charm bracelet, I had the poem for Gigi's Margaret copied and wrote a note to him to say I hoped he was well.

I have never maneuvered day-to-day life as others do, making
soups and dresses like Maman or ordering legions of resources
like Charles and Bobby's mother did. I am always well-pleased
simply to manage myself in the most rudimentary ways. I
mean, I remain hardy and reasonably dressed. I know how
to open a wine bottle and make coffee and tea and toast.
I use the telephone well, even these new mobile types that

respond to my voice and talk back on occasion. I forage for food in take-out places, delicatessens, and the like, or rely on a neighbor happy to cook for a fee as I did all my years in Newfoundland. I tell you this to explain why it was years before I mailed that poem to Gigi Paulo.

I just had no idea how to locate him.

~ 9 ~

During those many years that I was sorting Claire's apartment, I decided to help fund a rickety theater in the Village where the audience listened to plays over the rumble of the subway below, and I took to searching for first edition books that I could never have afforded before. Otherwise, I did not spend much money, did not cut the deals I had thought I might.

I watched my sculptors move on to another part of the city and Amy, the struggling actress, return home to teach school. I settled into a different sort of wandering and waiting, the rock cliffs of Saint John's replaced by the side streets of Manhattan, the wide spaces of exile exchanged then for a controlled deliberation over Claire's possessions. One year followed another. Politics changed. Restaurants opened and closed. My vintage watch kept time to the second, as Gigi had said that it would.

Nearing the end of my massive endeavor on Claire's behalf, I went to a meeting at the attorney's offices, where we were to finally discuss the sale of her things and the apartment itself and how that would all work to my benefit. I had maintained a cordial rapport with this group for a decade, keeping a certain aesthetic distance. I still did not quite trust that they wouldn't leap out of the audience and storm the stage. They were attorneys, after all.

At this meeting, a new young man came in with a fat file of papers under his arm and introduced himself as Edgar something-or-other. He reminded me of Bobby in his easy self-confidence, a kind of loose swagger when he moved. He'd probably gone to the same prep school and had a mother who ran half the city. He shook my hand, sat across from me, and crossed his long legs just the way Bobby once did.

"So," he said and began to explain the steps in finally selling the last of Claire's possessions.

"I'd like to call you Eddie," I interrupted.

He looked up from the file, then grinned. "Mrs. Bernard, you may call me whatever you choose. You are famous in my world, you know."

"And what world is that?" I replied.

"Law students study you. At least my class did. The abused wife who killed her husband and calmly walked out of the courtroom never to be heard of again for thirty-eight years. You are historic. In fact, I did a paper on the likelihood that you would have been convicted."

"And would I have been?"

"Yes," he answered and laughed. "Definitely."

"That's what I thought too," I said. "But I never think I killed Charles exactly. I do not arrange it that way in my mind."

He leaned across the table. "How do you arrange it?" He was not being coy. He really did want to know. And so I told him.

"I won."

He nodded slowly, as though agreeing with my thinking.

"I have no remorse," I went on. "One of us was bound to lose and I decided that morning in our kitchen it would not be me."

He leaned back away from me. "You want more coffee?"

I did want more coffee. I enjoyed talking to this Bobby-like character named after a Shakespearean prince. And after my favorite ghoul Poe as well. "Do you like your job here?" I asked. "Do you like being a junior attorney?"

The grin again. "Of course," he said.

In an instant, there in that posh conference room, I envisioned how this young man could manage the details of my life—not just Claire's estate, but buying my decrepit building on East Second Street, which I wanted to do, and not just that but watching over all these assets or deals I might seek or other people I might hire and keeping me up-to-date on a computer or whatever. Finding Gigi Paulo even.

I asked him. "Would you like to manage my life? Not just legal but operational, as they say. Financial and business things. Flexible hours," I added and smiled.

Edgar did not smile back. He sat thinking for some time, then said, "I'd like to seriously consider it, Mrs. Bernard. Perhaps we could arrange it under the umbrella of this office."

I shrugged at that. "Whatever umbrella you like, Eddie."

We spent an hour then on Claire's estate and nearly another hour on my life in exile, which he listened to with the rapture of a child caught in high adventure, although why I cannot say, as I did nearly nothing in exile. But youth still dreams.

As I stood up to leave, I said, "Tell me again how the law students think of me."

"You're famous," he answered.

"Yes."

"You are, Mrs. Bernard."

I fluffed my hair and lifted my shoulders. "Good to know," I replied.

Several months later I hired Eddie to run things for me. And several months after that, he found Gigi. In the late fall of 2011, I mailed the poem "Spring and Fall: To a Young Child" with my note. I did not include a return address, because I did not think it necessary.

Gigi knew where I lived.

~ 10 ~

That was a curious era, that time after hiring Eddie to help me. Claire's apartment went up for sale, and I began the process of purchasing my old building, which had become home to me. Eddie thought I should move to Claire's, arguing the advantages of location and value, the perfectly groomed rooms just waiting for me. But I preferred my place on East Second Street with its boarded fireplaces, iron radiators, and odd nooks here and there throughout, its wooden floors and ceiling painted white some decades ago, now chipped and peeling the way my apartment with Maman was back when. I could fix it to my liking. We could be decrepit together. And in idle hours I could look out at a quiet, insignificant street with its few struggling trees.

I did not have the old money of Bobby's family, but I then knew the deep cushion that Claire had rested upon all her life. I knew a sense of establishment. Even purpose. Now that I was done sorting Claire's life and had a professional to help manage my own, I sat down most days of the week to pen my story, the life of a wayfarer whose fate had been cast on the day she was born. It is something to have so many decades to roam, as though a small country had been parceled only for me to explore, to find its insurmountable hills and splash barefoot in its streams. *I grow old, I grow old, I shall wear the bottoms of my trousers rolled. Shall I put my hair behind? Do I dare to eat a peach? I shall wear white flannel trousers and walk upon the beach.*

I prepared for this next phase of my life, this time of aging and comfort. White flannel trousers, as it were. But I did not hear back from Gigi Paulo.

I had no illusion that we would change our destinies, but I had reached out to no avail and that irritated me. "Spring and Fall" is a haunting poem. He should have loved it. He should have found me again.

Eddie had given me a phone number for Gigi, which I tried several times throughout that winter. The phone rang without answer and no recording asked me to leave a message. Then when I called again in late March, a woman answered, her voice smooth but hesitant, even guarded.

"Who is this?" I asked.

"This is Gigi Paulo's daughter. Who is calling?"

"You are Margaret?"

"I am. Who are you? Who am I speaking to?"

"I am an old friend," I answered. "Your father is well? He is there?" She did not answer. The silence between us hung large. "Hello, Margaret?"

"My father died last November."

I had not even considered this possibility. In my mind Gigi Paulo would live well for at least one hundred years, breathing the air off his thousands of lakes and standing tall and handsome through time. Stunned, I asked, "How did this happen? I cannot imagine."

"He got sick. We never knew because he wouldn't see a doctor. He refused. So we don't know."

I cannot tell you how much I admired Gigi for that. Perhaps he had not been so different from me. Perhaps he had been more fierce and uncanny than I had thought. "Were you there?" I found myself wanting to picture what had happened. Everyone in my life had died away from me. I wanted a last picture.

"He called me to come and see him. He lives by a lake. Lived by the lake here. So I drove up from my home in Minneapolis and he was very sick. So I stayed. I made tea," she said, this daughter of his. "I made tea and then he fell asleep and then he was gone." Her voice broke.

"Did he read the poem I sent him? I sent him a beautiful poem for you."

"No, it came two weeks late. I read it."

"Did you keep it?" The poem I sent was about loss, in fact. *Margaret, are you grieving*—"I sent it for you."

She hesitated. "I read it. And the other note too. You told him not to find you. He kept that note. He kept it for the rest of his life."

Of course, he did. "I believe your father was in love with me for many years," I answered. I thought she should know.

But she did not seem to want to know. "Leave me alone," she said. "Please." Her voice wavered, but she did not hang up.

I did not hang up either. I was adjusting to this news that I'd lost another person who had known me and might have come back to me in some way. There was a night at Gigi's apartment when we had finished a soup he'd made for me and drunk all his cheap red wine as well. One of his lyrical crooners sang on the phonograph, and I asked him if he wanted to dance. I had never danced with a man before, but we moved about quite nicely, Gigi and I did, glancing down at our feet as though watching would make them glide more gracefully. "I've never known anyone like you," he said to me that night.

"I know," I answered.

"I don't think I ever will," he added.

Now there was only his Margaret breathing into the phone, as alone as I was. Who is the child standing across the way, balanced on the edge between the pebbles and tall weeds? Who waves first? Who waves in return?

"My name is Corrine Bernard, Margaret. Your father almost saved me once, but then he chose not to. Even so I never forget him."

She remained silent, and then I realized she had stopped the call at some point, though I did not know when.

The day had seemed to fade in that short while I talked with Gigi's Margaret. I turned on a lamp, poured myself a glass of very old port, and stood looking out at the narrow street before me. The trees remained bare from the long winter, the passersby purposeful. At the end of the day, we gather up what is left of our frivolities and go home, do we not? No need to blame the clouds or the angle of the sun, the grasses too high or the river too low.

We all have our times.
And we have our tales.

These are mine, dear reader. These are mine.